WHAT BAD BITCHES DO

Lock Down Publications and Ca$h
Presents

What Bad Bitches Do

A Novel by *Aryanna*

Lock Down Publications
P.O. Box 870494
Mesquite, Tx 75187

Visit our website @
www.lockdownpublications.com

First Edition June 2018
Printed in the United States of America

Lock Down Publications
Like our page on Facebook: Lock Down Publications @
www.facebook.com/lockdownpublications.ldp
Cover design and layout by: **Dynasty Cover Me**
Book interior design by: **Shawn Walker**
Edited by: **Jill Alicea**

Stay Connected with Us!

Text **LOCKDOWN** to 22828 to stay up-to-date with new releases, sneak peaks, contests and more…
Or **CLICK HERE** to sign up.
Thank you.

Like our page on Facebook:

Lock Down Publications: Facebook

Join Lock Down Publications/The New Era Reading Group

Visit our website @ www.lockdownpublications.com

Follow us on Instagram:

Lock Down Publications: Instagram

Email Us: We want to hear from you!

Submission Guideline

Submit the first three chapters of your completed manuscript to ldpsubmissions@gmail.com, subject line: Your book's title. The manuscript must be in a .doc file and sent as an attachment. Document should be in Times New Roman, double spaced and in size 12 font. Also, provide your synopsis and full contact information. If sending multiple submissions, they must each be in a separate email.

Have a story but no way to send it electronically? You can still submit to LDP/Ca$h Presents. Send in the first three chapters, written or typed (DO NOT USE FRONT AND BACK OF PAPER), of your completed manuscript to:

LDP: Submissions Dept
Po Box 870494
Mesquite, Tx 75187

DO NOT send original manuscript. Must be a duplicate.

Provide your synopsis and a cover letter containing your full contact information.

Thanks for considering LDP and Ca$h Presents.

CHAPTER ONE
IVY
Jan 2018

"EB, I'm out front, bring your ass," I demanded, hanging up before she could get a word out in response.

This bitch was *always* late, like my arrival was some unexpected visit from a distant relative. No doubt I loved her crazy ass like a sister, but if she kept this shit up, she'd be walking to school instead of riding shotgun in my silver Aston Martin. It was still another three months before this high yellow heifer came strutting out her front door, like she was about to hit a runway in NY's fashion week instead of a classroom on Texas University campus.

"All that cuteness gonna get your ass left," I warned once she was seated beside me.

"Okay, first of all my name is EB-O-NY, like the black queen I am, so please stop shortening it. And secondly, you know we don't make public appearances anything less than all the way put together, as evidenced by that hip-hugging little Versace number you have on."

"Bitch, please, you ain't even dark enough to have the name Ebony," I replied, laughing and pulling away from her townhouse.

"Light-skinned I may be, but these hips, tits, and ass are black genetics without a doubt," she replied, laughing too.

There was definite truth in that statement because homegirl was *thick* with all capital letters. She was only about an inch taller than my 5'4" height, but we weighed around the same at 150 pounds, which was mostly curves. Never would we be mistaken for twins though because I was licorice black and proud of it, plus we possessed different kinds of beauty.

Ebony had that almost flawless, classic model look, especially when she straightened her natural curls, but it was understandable given her mixed heritage. Me, on the other hand, with my high cheekbones, short hairdo, and smooth black skin, I was that New Age edgy type model, but that wasn't really my thing. I wore certain clothes because they looked good on me, but EB wanted to flaunt her status. Better yet, her parents' status.

"When your pops giving you your car back anyway? I'm tired of being your chauffeur," I said teasingly.

"You know how that nigga is once he sets his mind to something, so I'm not even 'bout to ask him. And stop acting like we don't go everywhere together anyway, bitch."

"True. It has been six months though. I mean, how long is he gonna be mad?" I asked seriously.

"You weren't there that night. I ain't never seen him that mad at me before. I'm as big a daddy's girl as you are, but when he slapped the spit out of my mouth I knew we were on another level of anger. Looking back now I know it wasn't so much the DUI that had him pissed, but the fact that I'd gotten caught, which brought police and unwanted heat on the family."

Looking at it from that perspective, I could completely understand how her dad felt. Our fathers were in the game together, so I knew hers had taught her just like mine had taught me that you didn't do dumb shit that could bring the cops to your door. It didn't matter how many police or local politicians they had on the payroll because you didn't go to the well until you were dying of thirst. I've done my fair share of dirt, but to society, I was nothing more than a twenty-two-year-old college kid with a 3.5 GPA. Even though Ebony was a year older, she still had lapses in judgement, but she was my ace and I'd ride with her till the end.

"Well look at the bright side, at least he didn't take your house and make you move back home," I said.

"That's only because him and mom like to walk around butt ass naked and fuck everywhere."

"Eww! That's *too* much info," I exclaimed, fighting to keep my car on the road while blocking the visual imagery she'd put in my mind.

"If I gotta know, you gotta know. We family," she replied, laughing.

"Nah, keep that shit to yourself, bitch, I don't wanna know. Ugh!"

"Shit will give you nightmares, I'm telling you. Anyways, where was your ass last night?" she asked, pulling out her compact to check her make-up.

"You know it was Sunday, which means dinner at the big house."

"You know when you say it like that it sounds like a plantation house, right?"

"Shit, it probably was at one point considering all the land it sits on, and this *is* Texas," I replied, acknowledging the tortured history and deep-seeded hatred that still existed in the Lone Star State.

"How'd dinner go? Did Rita cook?"

"You know she did. I swear I ate so many BBQ ribs that I was cross-eyed by the time I got up from the table."

"I thought your dress looked tighter than usual," she said, laughing.

"Fuck you, bitch, you're just like me when it comes to eating, so shut up."

"True. For real though, how's Rita doing? I thought she was supposed to be taking it easy."

"You know nurses and doctors make the worst patients, and to quote my mother, 'ain't no cancer gonna slow me down'," I replied, shaking my head.

"That sounds like your mom. She'll be alright though."

We both knew she was lying, but it was one of those acceptable lies because it was told to help and not hurt. The cancer had spread too far to turn back now and so, like the proud woman she was, my mom was determined to live and die on her own terms. That meant living every day like normal, which was more than difficult for my father and me, but we'd do anything to make her happy. Only those close to me knew how much this was truly affecting me because I'd been down this road before. My birth mother died long before I knew how to mourn or even remember, but when Margarita came into the picture when I was nine years old, she helped me with both. From that point on, our bond was forged in a way that was unbreakable because I found a mother and friend that I could count on forever. The only problem is that forever doesn't last that long.

"Is that who I think it is?" Ebony asked as I pulled into a parking space next to a money green 2018 Escalade sitting high on thirty-two-inch rims.

Before I could answer, the back door opened and a man we both knew stepped out into the bright morning sunlight. To the streets he was known as Big Cuzz, and given his 6'5" height with his 250 pound frame, most people understood why. The reality was that his OG status carried more weight than his game and he was nothing to fuck with, but he was my teddy bear.

"This is a surprise," I said, stepping out of the car and into his waiting embrace.

"I know, but I had some business down here, so I decided to swing through."

"You mean pop up, like you expected me to be doing something naughty," I replied, jabbing him slightly in the ribs. I looked up to find him smiling down at me, but it wasn't quite reaching his eyes. To everyone else I knew he appeared completely normal - just an attractive brown-skinned brother with low cut hair and a scruffy chin strap - but I knew how dangerous his mind was. Added to that was the fact that he was a long way from Houston, and if he was way out here, that meant he had business with our dads.

"How long are you staying?" I asked.

"I don't know yet, but I've got plans for you," he replied suggestively.

"Babe, you know I've got class."

"And I know Ebony can take notes," he insisted, stepping back from me to open the door to his truck so I could climb in. I turned to find EB giving me a nod of approval, prompting me to grab my bag and toss her my keys.

"You drink and drive my shit, bitch, and I'ma kill you. I'm *not* playing," I warned.

"You *know* I'm not 'bout to do that shit again. I got you. Just go have fun, but remember, we have that fundraiser tonight for Professor Jessup's class."

"I'll be there," I replied before hopping into the backseat next to my man. I was surprised by the fact that it was just Big and his driver because he never traveled this light, especially when he was away from his base of operations.

"Where are we going?" I asked.

"To your place. And you won't need these," he replied, reaching beneath my dress and snatching my panties off.

It looked like I was still gonna get some learning after all.

CHAPTER 2
SOLOMAN

"How are you feeling, sweetheart?"

"I'd be feeling better if you wouldn't coddle me and - "

"So now it's coddling for a man to fix his wife breakfast in bed?" I asked.

"I guess not," she replied, giving me a sheepish smile as I removed the now-empty tray from her lap and set it on the nightstand.

It was good to see her with a healthy appetite, and I did my best to keep my smile in place while my mind flashed forward to the days when I wouldn't be able to do this for her. She didn't want my pity or my sadness, and my love outweighed both, so I wouldn't upset her. I would simply do as I've always done and make the most of every moment we had left.

"Now, without the smart-ass commentary, how are you really feeling?" I asked again.

"Horny," she replied, throwing the covers back to reveal her nakedness.

I'd heard stories about how cancer ravaged the body, but in my mind, Margarita Campos was still the most beautiful woman I'd ever seen. Even at thirty-five she had the bronze-colored skin of a twenty-year-old. Standing 5'3" with those voluptuous curves every man fantasizes about navigating, she never failed to turn me on. In truth, it wasn't her gorgeous body though. It was her eyes. I'd never met a Puerto Rican woman with natural blue eyes, and from the moment I first looked into them, I was lost to her - as lost as I was right now.

"You know I can satisfy more than one appetite," I said, opening my robe and letting it drop to reveal my equally naked body.

“Prove it,” she challenged, opening her legs wide for me to look deep into one of my favorite places.

“Mmm, I am hungry,” I purred, climbing onto the bed and pulling her towards me.

Like a man with tunnel vision, I locked onto her clit and sucked it until I felt her back arch up off the bed, pinning her arms to her side and forcing her to ride the wave of her building climax with no hands. I teased her for several minutes, alternating between forceful sucking, quick flicks of my tongue across her most sensitive gumdrop, and long, lazy licks from the crack of her beautiful ass upward.

“Wh-why are you s-so cruel?” she asked breathlessly.

“Because you taste good. Delicious, in fact,” I replied, going right back to my meal.

“Sol-Soloman, please!” she begged.

I was no longer listening to her words though because I was only hearing the sweet melody her body was humming. I knew what she wanted, but this was my show for the moment, so I continued my onslaught of licks until I felt the uncontrollable shaking begin.

“Oh, oh, Soloman, I love…I love…”

“I know,” I said, moving swiftly from kneeling in between her legs to aligning our bodies for the next phase.

With my first pounding blow inside her, I felt the skies open and her rain all over me in a powerful surge. No matter how many times we did this, the feelings and sensations I got from being inside her, from being one with her, felt completely brand new. Even with her cumming hard enough to make her beautiful blue eyes roll into the back of her head, I still maintained the force of the strokes I was delivering, motivated by the sounds of wetness echoing off the wall. Words were no longer possible for her, but her moans and screams made my spine tingle as much as the feeling of her pussy walls collapsing around my dick every time I dove deep. I didn't wanna cum, but she was making it damn near impossible for me to hold on.

"B-baby, you c-can't - " The rest of the words were lost in my throat because she'd locked her legs behind my back and now had the leverage to lift her hips up into the punishment I was giving.

"Fuck," I panted weakly as my eyes lost focus and I came with earth-stopping intensity.

Not to be outdone, she climaxed again right behind me with a high-pitched scream to punctuate the occasion. I was too weak to think about moving, but that was fine with my beautiful wife because she loved when we could cuddle like this.

"I th-think you were trying t-to kill me," I mumbled, fighting to catch my breath, but still smiling from ear to ear.

"Likewise. I'm gonna get my wins when I can with you or you'll fuck the walls straight out of my pussy."

"You know you like it when I go deep," I whispered, kissing her tenderly.

"No. I love it, just like I love you, Soloman."

"And I love you too, sweetheart, always and forever."

At first, I thought I said the wrong thing because tears appeared in her eyes instantly, but there was a genuine smile that accompanied them. This time when I kissed her it was with renewed passion, but unlike our first round, I wanted to take it slow and steady. For the next half hour we stayed locked in the same embrace, hearts beating in sync, as I gave her slow, thorough strokes until we both banged on death's door in ecstasy. This time when it was over I moved off of her so I could pull her close and let her fall back to sleep in my arms.

I had no doubt that she probably thought this action was purely for her benefit, but she was really just giving me another memory to add to the collections I would cherish long after she was gone. Before I knew it, an hour had passed with me holding her and watching her sleep, and I would've been content to continue laying here. But I had business to handle. Being an OG in the game didn't mean your work load decreased or you didn't have as many things to worry about. It was actually the opposite. When you were the head, it was your responsibility to make sure the rest of the body functioned properly, which was why two heads were always better than one. At the age of fifty, I understood that my survival and success wasn't because of dumb luck or because I knew all the answers to the questions. I had a partner, someone to counter-balance the weakness that exists in us all, and someone to share in making sure half of the body didn't become paralyzed due to neglect. In my mind, when you had someone like that, then the game really didn't have an expiration date until Father Time came calling.

Moving in stealth, I got up from the bed, put my robe back on, and made my way to the guest bedroom to shower. Twenty minutes later I was refreshed and dressed in a black tailor-made suit, ready to face the world's uncertainties with the cold calculation needed to survive. After writing Rita a note telling her that I loved her and would be home for dinner, I gave her a gentle kiss and made my way outside to the waiting 2019 Lincoln Continental.

"Where to, Mr. Black?" my driver asked.

"Take me to the Galveston port," I ordered, pulling my phone out and texting Jacob to let him know I was on the way.

Truthfully, the last thing I wanted to be doing was conducting business, but there was no way Rita would let me stay around the house all day hovering over her. She was too independent, and too damn mean, for that. One would think that with the type of power I commanded, especially amongst those I associated with, that I could win an argument with my wife. Nah; she'd come at me all the way logical and explain that the empire didn't crumble because the queen was sick. That was weakness, and she hadn't married a weak nigga.

A sudden alert came through my phone that had my blood pressure rising fast because Ivy *knew* better than to skip school. I was two digits away from calling her when I got a text from her saying she was with Big Cuzz, and that made me pause. I should've figured he'd stop and see her to make sure she was safe, despite the eyes I had on her full time. There were always dangers and threats that came with this business, but there was something new in the air that had us all concerned. There was no such thing as coincidence, so the fact that a couple of our major dope and money shipments got knocked meant there was a weak link in the chain. Added to that was the cartel violence that was spilling over from my partners in Mexico, which gave me even more incentive to tighten up security. It was these topics that were the focus of the meeting I was en route to, and hopefully we could figure out how to fix the problems.

I spent the five hour drive reaching out to my various business interests, making sure that things were running as smooth as possible. By the time I arrived at the port in Galveston, I'd distributed ten million dollars around to secure the fifty million I had on the move. It really did take money to make money.

"Be ready to leave within an hour," I said to my driver, stepping from the car and making my way to the permanent office I kept here to oversee my biggest investment.

It wasn't often that I got to make the trip out here anymore, but that was okay because Jacob was just as efficient as I was, and just as ruthless.

"Good afternoon, gentlemen," I said, greeting both Jacob and our Sinaloa Cartel connect José.

"What's going on, black man," Jacob responded, shaking my hand and pulling me into a half hug.

Jacob and I could easily pass for brothers because of our dark skin tone and similar facial features, but I was a couple inches taller. We both towered over José, but the 5'5" Mexican exuded power from his compact stature, and I respected that. José simply nodded and continued to puff on his cigar. Both of the men knew my distaste for smoke, but it seemed like a trivial argument to have in the face of bigger problems.

"Let's get down to business," I said, taking a seat across from José at the cheap conference table that took up a lot of space in the small office. Jacob sat down beside me, fixing his eyes on our silent partner as well.

"You're losing money," José stated.

"I'm aware," I replied calmly.

"That's unacceptable for us. So what do you plan to do?" José asked.

"We all know this is a business of wins and losses, and the trick is to win more than you lose. We do that. To expect absolutely no loss is unreasonable," Jacob said.

"Losing 100 million in both product and money in the last ninety days is unreasonable. In fact, it looks completely incompetent," José replied through a cloud of smoke.

I cast a quick glance in Jacob's direction, expecting to find some clue that Jose's numbers were exaggerated, but my man had his poker face screwed on tight.

"We're in the process of fixing the problem, and you already know the money isn't coming out of your pocket either way," Jacob assured him.

"That's not the point. You're overlooking the fact that it makes your business look weak, vulnerable. That will make others test the waters and it could even cost you your protection from la policia," José reasoned.

"The killings and kidnapping's spilling over from Mexico into Texas could cause us to lose our police protection. How about you put a stop to that?" I suggested.

"People die; people will always die. It's inevitable. We do what must be done to maintain control," José stated matter-of-factly.

"Look, are we gonna keep pushing blame, or come up with viable solutions? Because I have other business to handle," I said, becoming frustrated.

"The solution is you handle your business, or we'll handle it for you. And until you get a handle on shit, the well is dry," José said.

"You know, you're not the only game in town with dope," I replied, calling his bluff.

"No, I'm not, but I'm the wrong person to disrespect by trying to go around me."

"So, you expect me to do what? Lose my clientele? Jacob just told you that we've got the situation under control," I said.

"I know what Jacob said, and if that's true, then you'll have everything straight before you run out of product. In the meantime, we can handle a different type of business to ensure money still flows both ways," José suggested, putting his cigar out in the coffee cup in front of him.

"What business?" I asked.

"Due to President Trump's rants about immigration it's hard to get people here, so - "

"I told you before we're not getting into the human trafficking business," I replied firmly.

"You sure about that? Maybe you should talk it over with Jacob, considering he's already accepted payment for the first run," José said, smiling.

I didn't even have to turn and look at the man next to me because I could feel him tense up as soon as the truth was spoken. Stupid mu'fucka made a deal with the devil.

CHAPTER 3
EBONY

"Ms. Dahl, can I speak to you really quick?"

"Sure, Professor Jessup," I replied, putting my iPad in my bag and moving to the front of the class as everyone filed out.

"I noticed Ms. Black wasn't in class today. Is everything alright?"

"Oh, she's fine, just had some personal matters to attend to."

"So does that mean I can still expect you two to help with tonight's event?" he asked hopefully.

"Of course. We wouldn't miss it. Social activism is high on both of our priority lists, and breast cancer awareness is close to both of our hearts."

"I'm grateful for both of you young ladies' support. The fundraiser dinner begins at 7:30 p.m. in the banquet hall, but you should arrive at least a half an hour early to help with any last minute details. Will yours and Ms. Black's parents be attending?"

"I'm not sure, but I know they've all made generous donations," I replied, pulling my vibrating phone out of my bag.

"Okay, well I'll let you go and I'll see you tonight."

I heard his words, but I was too distracted by the message telling me to come out front.

I knew the number, but pop-up visits were extremely rare, and two in the same day was unheard of. Something was definitely up. Slinging my bag over my shoulder, I quickly made my way to the parking lot, where I found my own man leaned against Ivy's car.

"Okay, what's *really* going on?" I asked, stopping in front of him.

"Damn, it's good to see you too, bae. Don't I get a better welcome than that?"

I couldn't resist the urge to simply melt into his massive body, loving how we fit together despite him being 6'4" and 320 pounds. Rock, short for Rockafella, was every bit as intimidating as they come in appearance, and for good reason because he had no hesitation for fucking a nigga up. But with me he was gentle, and I loved that. I gave him a big hug and an even bigger kiss, but I backed away before either of us could get caught up in the moment.

"Alright, explain," I demanded.

"What's to explain? I missed you, so I came to scoop you up for the weekend."

"Nah, my nigga, you don't do shit like that without hitting me up to make sure I don't got nothing going on first. Plus, Big is down here too, and he said the trip was about business," I concluded, folding my arms over my ample chest and giving him my resting bitch face.

Immediately he smiled in an effort to disarm me, but I could tell by the look in his eyes that he knew not to feed me no more bullshit.

"Come on, take a ride with me and I'll explain," he said, gesturing towards the black on black 2018 Mercedes E class coupe parked next to us.

"I can't. I gotta drive Ivy's car."

"You what? Ebony, you ain't - "

"I know I ain't got no license, but Big showed up here and they left before we even made it to the building. Stop giving me that damn look and just follow me to my house," I said, digging the keys out of my bag and moving around him to unlock the door.

I could still feel his penetrating gaze following my movements, but by the time I was behind the wheel with the engine started, he was in his car. I understood no matter how old I got, I'd have to deal with my father's judgement, over protectiveness, and all-around bullshit, but sometimes Rock pissed me off when I got it from him too. I knew he was only looking out for me, but I was a big girl capable of making good choices and learning from the bad ones. Just to be a smart ass I sped the whole way to my place and made the thirty minute drive in half the time.

Before getting out of the car, I sent Ivy a text letting her know that her car handled like a dream and asking what the *fuck* was going on because Rock was in town too. Once Rock pulled up beside me I got out and led the way into the house, ignoring the pissed looks he was tossing my way.

"You want something to drink?" I offered.

"Yeah, let me get a mimosa."

Now it was my turn to give him an ugly look because he knew I'd given up drinking and didn't allow the shit in my house either.

"Whatever, nigga, you'll have a Coke and a smile, so sit your ass on the couch," I said, putting down my bag and going to the kitchen. When I came back into the living room I found him stretched out on the couch with his hands behind his head.

"Oh, so you think this is about to be a therapy session?" I asked, setting his soda on the table and taking the adjourning loveseat.

"Nah, just trying to organize my thoughts. I apologize for telling you a half-truth earlier," he replied, sitting up to face me.

"Yeah, what's up with that? We don't lie to each other."

"We don't discuss business either. I know that you and Ivy know what we're all into, but we do our best to keep you ignorant to a lot of shit so your hands remain clean. This situation's different."

"Different how?" I asked, more intrigued than worried.

It had never been a secret between me and Ivy about how our fathers had gotten to where they were. It had actually made our bond stronger because we were part of something not many understood. Still, we were kept away from any dirt or bullshit that could blow back on us, and like most kids with parents like ours, we preferred it that way. Neither of us wanted to be in the game, despite the fact that we loved and accepted our men for who they were.

"I can't give you too many details, and some of what I'm about to say is common knowledge anyway. The drama in Mexico is getting worse. That, I'm sure you've seen all over the news. That's affecting business, but it's not the only thing because a couple shipments have been hit too."

"Isn't that part of it?" I asked, still not understanding whether to be scared or not.

"Yeah, it's normally part of it, but this is too much of a loss to go ignored, and we can't afford to keep letting it happen."

"Stop dancing around whatever it is you're not saying, because even though I'm not in your business, I know enough to know that losses come with the territory. Even big losses."

"We think someone's moving against us," he said calmly.

"That's part of it too, so - "

"Yeah it is, but most mu'fuckas try to take over areas so they can push their own product. This feels like someone is trying to dismantle the whole operation, which puts everyone in danger. Just because Sol and Jacob run shit don't mean that they don't got people to answer to, and these ain't people any of us wanna fuck with," he stated plainly.

I was beginning to understand what had brought both him and Big Cuzz all the way from Houston on such short notice. Big was Hoover Crip, and Rock was part of the Global

Gangsta movement, which meant they both had armies behind them and us. Somehow after hearing what he had to say I was getting the feeling that their homies might not be enough, and that *did* scare me.

"So what happens now?" I asked.

"Big and me had to come sit down with Sol and your dad face to face to compare information and shit. They're having a meeting with their partners, and then after that we'll all sit down again. Until then, I just wanna spend time with you, and after my meeting, I want you to go back to Houston with me."

"For how long?"

"Do it matter? You gonna be with me so that's time well spent," he replied, smiling seductively.

"As enticing as that sounds, you know I can't just drop everything and skate out of town with you. I've got an important fundraiser to attend tonight, as a matter of fact."

"That's cool. I'll be your plus one," he said, winking at me.

The thing about Rock was that despite his size, he did blend well because he kept his appearance neat and clean. His beard stayed trimmed and lined up, and the low cut kept the waves in full rotation. All he'd really need was some formal wear because the jeans and T-shirt look wouldn't fly.

"You ain't got shit to wear," I said, looking him up and down.

"Oh, so you got rid of the clothes I've been keeping here? Why, you got another nigga you dealing with?" If he hadn't asked this question with a smile on his face, I would've been calling him everything except Jesus and Judas, but the smile got a pillow thrown at him instead.

"Nigga, you know your clothes are upstairs, but this is a *formal* event and nothing you got fits the bill."

"Guess I need to go shopping. Can I get a little kiss first, and maybe get some of your time?" he asked, smiling in that all too familiar way that always resulted in me losing my panties.

I got up and gave him the kiss he requested, but I backed up before he could lock his big arms around me.

"Why you playing?" he asked, reaching for me again.

"First you go get your outfit while I take a nice, relaxing bubble bath to wash the day's funk away, and then we'll talk about you getting some of my time."

'Come on, bae - "

"You're wasting time, Rockafella, time that you might want later," I said, equally seductive.

We both knew that he had the gift of gab, but he knew that arguing with me was pointless. Pussy ran the world and all of the powerful men in it, and I'd learned that from my mother during our birds and bees convo way back when.

"A'ight, I'ma go get something really quick, but you better stay your ass in this house while I'm gone," he demanded.

I opened my mouth with a smart-ass retort on the tip of my tongue, but I could see this was a serious moment.

"I'm not taking my ass anywhere except to the marble claw foot tub upstairs."

"Good. I'll be back, and you better be naked when I get here," he said, getting up and heading for the door.

My pussy was already screaming at me for not getting a quick round in, but now it was throbbing because I loved when he handled me rough both verbally and physically. I followed him to the door and locked it behind him since he had a key. Grabbing my phone out of my bag, I made my way up to my bedroom, sending Ivy another text telling her what time to be back at campus for the event. I wasn't surprised she hadn't hit me back yet because if I knew her, she had her hands as full as mine would be in a short while. With the immediate business out of the way, I got down to my birthday suit and filled my tub with hot water followed by something a little sweet-smelling that kept my honey skin irresistibly soft.

"Now this is what a bitch *needed*," I exclaimed aloud, stepping into the water and taking a seat.

Immediately I began to decompress and feel the waves of relaxation fly over me, but sooner than expected I heard my front door open and Rock calling my name loudly.

"I'm up here!" I yelled back, not moving from my position beneath the millions of bubbles.

"Get out the tub."

"I'm not done, I - "

"Get the fuck out of the tub! We gotta go," he ordered, almost frantically.

"Wh-what's wrong? Rock, what is it?"

"It's war."

CHAPTER 4
JACOB

Here I sat next to my oldest friend in the world, wondering why the fuck the truth never stayed buried as long as we wanted it to. Winston Churchill said a lie would get halfway around the world before the truth had a chance to put its pants on. Right now, the race was too close to call. Sol was my brother, and the major part of our success was only possible because of trust and loyalty. And honesty. We didn't lie or bullshit with each other, and most of the time we moved in step because we thought the same way on everything that was important. Until now. Since only eight months separated us in age, I'd never used the fact that I was older to dispense wisdom or as an excuse to feel like I knew more than he did. The fact of the matter was that times were changing, and I could see that clearly, but Soloman lacked vision, and so in order for us to thrive, I had to make the tough decisions.

"What's he talking about, Jacob?" Soloman asked.

"Listen, Sol, the game is changing. We got a president now who's saying there's an opioid epidemic, and that means mu'fuckas getting caught up is getting body rocked at trial. What that means is they're talking deals, and the more mu'fuckas that fold, the more dangerous it is for us."

"And you think trafficking people, human beings, is gonna be somehow better for us if we get caught?" he asked in disbelief and growing frustration.

"It's more lucrative and - "

"Nigga, it's contributing to the slave trade! Are you that fucking blind that you can't see that?!" he roared, pounding his fist on the table.

"Are you really trying to get on some holier than thou shit, nigga, like slanging metric tons of heroin and cocaine ain't enslaving people and fucking up families? Either way we got blood on our hands and we'll always have blood on our hands, but I'm smart enough to lower the risk of us going to prison for what we do."

For a moment we all sat in silence, each of us dealing with the truth in our own way. José and I had had many calmer conversations about this exact topic and we both felt the same way, especially given the competition to corner the dang market in Mexico. There was easier money to be made by providing safe passage into the U.S. and then extorting both money and favors from those you helped, in exchange for their family's protection back home. I just needed to convince Sol of this.

"It'll work, Sol. All we have to do - "

"You must didn't hear me when I said this to José, so I'll say it slowly. We're not – trafficking – people."

"It's unfortunate that you're taking this position. I'd hoped you'd see the bigger picture," José said, pulling out his phone and sending a text.

"Thanks, but no thanks. We'll handle business as we always have, and we'll fix the issues we've been having. Assure your boss of this," Soloman said, standing up to show he was done with the meeting.

"Oh, my boss has already been reassured," José replied just as the door behind us opened.

Turning around, I found two men big enough to dwarf both my 6'1" and Sol's 6'3" height, and the looks on their faces said this business was far from concluded.

"What the fuck do you think this is?" Soloman asked the two men before turning back to face José.

"As I told you, amigo, the deal has already been brokered and accepted."

"Yeah, well, my partner made a mistake and now you know what it is," Soloman replied confidently.

"Why don't I let Jacob tell you what it is?" José said, standing as well.

"Jacob?" Soloman questioned.

I hated being in this position, but I knew if Sol just had time to think then he'd see reason.

"There's no going back, but I understand that you need time to come around to our way of thinking. I'll handle everything, and I've been assured you'll be kept in comfort," I said.

"Comfort? What the fuck are you talking 'bout, kept - "

His question was silenced by the quick blow to the back of his head that rendered him unconscious, but the second man caught him before he could hit the floor.

"What about the driver?" José asked.

"Already taken care of, Jefe," the man replied, carrying Soloman back out the way they'd just come.

Part of me couldn't believe what I'd allowed to happen, but I pushed all those emotions from the front of my mind to focus on the bigger picture.

"We good?" José asked, lighting another cigar and puffing on it slowly.

"As long as no harm comes to him, we're good."

"Have you thought about what you will do if he never comes around to our way of thinking, amigo?'

"He'll come around. He's a businessman," I replied, hoping my voice didn't give away the lack of confidence I truly felt.

Soloman was indeed a businessman, but he was also a stubborn son of a bitch.

"Do you got your story straight for the family?" José asked.

"I'll handle everything on my end. You just do your part and shit will go smoothly."

"I certainly hope so, because you've got a lot riding on this. Maybe everything," José said, leaving me alone in the office with just my thoughts and betrayal for company.

Pulling out my phone, I sent Rock a text telling him to get my daughter to Houston immediately because Soloman had been kidnapped. I had no doubt that he'd handle that without question, but eventually I'd have to bring him into my confidence to ensure that I had his movement behind me.

This new business venture didn't come with the same risks as the dope game, but men in powerful positions always needed muscle to ensure that they could maintain those positions. With my daughter's safety secured, I quickly locked up the office and headed for my 2017 burgundy Maybach.

"Take me to the helipad," I ordered the driver, already texting my helicopter pilot to let him know our departure was immediate.

Within fifteen minutes I was in the air, and an hour later I was touching down in the backyard of my fourteen bedroom estate. Given the fact that Ebony was an only child, there had never really been a reason to have a house this big, but my wife Marissa came from old cattle money and she liked the finer things.

"How was your meeting?" she asked as soon as I came in through the back door that opened into the kitchen.

"As expected. What do you got going on?" I asked, kissing her on the cheek while peeking over her shoulder into the pans on the stove.

Marissa may have come from money, but this was still the south, and women got busy in the kitchen. Even white women weren't strangers to soul food.

"A little of this and a little of that. You'll just have to stick around if you really wanna know."

"You ain't gotta tell me twice. But make sure there's enough for your baby girl," I said.

"Ebony is coming? Why, what's wrong?" she asked, her spoon freezing in mid-air as worry quickly clouded her beautiful face.

It wasn't like Ebony didn't spend time with us just because she lived four hours away, but surprise visits normally signaled something of importance, and it was rarely good news.

"She's coming at my request," I replied, taking a seat on the bar stool across from my wife so I could talk to her without interrupting her cooking.

I knew what I had to say wouldn't be easy to hear because we were all like family, plus Marissa didn't completely agree with my lifestyle choices. In truth, the only reason she even tolerated my business is because I'd saved her father's life years ago by doing shit the police couldn't. That was years ago, and I was way more legit now than I was then, but it was moments like this where I knew she still hated the things I had to do.

"Okay, so why did you request her presence? Because we both knew that request means demand," Marissa said, setting her cooking spoon down and eyeing me closely.

"There's some shit going on and it's serious. More serious than it's ever been."

"Are we in danger, Jacob?"

"I'm handling it, and - "

"That's not what the fuck I asked you, and don't bullshit me either," she said forcefully.

"You know there's certain shit I can't tell you, but yes, there is danger lurking. I'm doing everything I can to protect our family, which was why I sent Rock to get Ebony earlier."

I could see her visibly relax when I said Ebony was with Rockafella because we both knew he'd put his life on the line for her without thinking twice.

"Okay, that's good. I'm sure you've already talked this over with Soloman, so all I wanna know is, can you two handle whatever this situation is?" she asked, picking the spoon back up.

I gave the proper amount of pause before answering because here's where shit got sticky. Marissa and I had been together since we were kids, so she'd always been able to smell my bullshit a mile away.

"I need to be honest with you, babe, but I can only do that if you promise not to break our number one rule," I said.

"Oh. This really is serious. But yes, I promise to not say or do anything that shows my emotions instead of my intellect."

"Soloman has been kidnapped."

At first it looked like my words hadn't penetrated her brain because she kept right on stirring the delicious-smelling food. Then suddenly she snapped, put her spoon down again, and walked out of the kitchen. I had no idea where she was going, but this behavior was completely new for her. I'd always kept both her and Ebony away from my business, but a lot I'd learned when it came to survival was applicable to all walks of life. You couldn't let your emotions determine your decisions. Only your intelligence should do that.

I had no idea what Marissa was thinking, but I didn't think she was gonna be able to keep her promise about rule number one. I was just about to get up and shut off the burners on the stove so the food didn't burn when my wife reappeared and did it herself.

"Babe, I know it's crazy and - "

My words were lost because I was now focused on the nickel-plated .45 she'd just pulled from her apron. It wasn't the first time I'd see the particular gun because Soloman had given it to her as a wedding present, with explicit instructions to shoot my dick off if I ever cheated.

"Explain to me how Soloman gets kidnapped and you're home in time for dinner," she demanded.

"Sweetheart, rule number one - "

"Oh, I'm not breaking any rules because both my intelligence and my emotions are saying we need to go get Soloman! But first you need to explain what – the – fuck – happened, Jacob."

Everybody who saw my wife thought she was simply Susie Homemaker, privileged and spoiled, but they didn't see this side of her. They didn't see the fire in her blue-green eyes, or the threat that her 5'6", 130 pound body posed. Most people didn't even know her. She was loyal, fiercely loyal, and God help those who fucked with anything she loved. I was gonna have to tread lightly on this one.

"We can't go at this situation with guns blazing because these people have more money and more power than us," I said.

"Wait, so you know who has him? I don't give a fuck what they have because what they really have is your best friend, and - "

"Shut up and listen!" I yelled, immediately getting her attention because I didn't normally talk to her this way. "This is about business and the people we do business with, the people we answer to. They're not gonna hurt Soloman, but they could, just like they could come after me and my family."

"So why didn't they? Why him?" she asked softly.

"Because I'm the one who agreed to do what they asked, and he didn't. We both knew the stakes, but Sol is stubborn sometimes. I don't know, maybe with all our years of success he felt like we were untouchable, but the bottom line is that everybody answers to somebody."

"So what happens now?"

"I'm gonna do what I gotta do to make the business work…and to bring Soloman home, one way or another."

CHAPTER 5
IVY

"Bae-Bae, you gotta let me concentrate if you wanna eat," I said, stirring the potatoes in the pan in front of me.

"Oh, I'm gonna eat," he replied, kissing my neck and slowly working his way lower.

There was a word for niggas like Big, and it was insatiable! From the time we'd come through the door of my condo, he'd been on me non-stop, but I wasn't complaining because he knew everything I liked. You would've thought that fucking up my headboard all day would've been enough, but nah, because here I was trying to cook us something to eat and he was walking his big juicy lips down my spine.

"Big, s-stop," I whined, knowing he wouldn't.

To no surprise he grabbed me by the waist and held me in one spot while he continued kissing lower and lower. By now it was an effort to keep the potatoes in the pan and duck the hot grease that was poppin' from the bacon and sausage in my other pan. I figured he'd stop once he reached my lower back, but when I felt his moist kisses begin covering my ass, I dropped the egg I'd just picked up.

"Gotta be more careful," he said, laughing softly, but still not loosening the grip he had on me.

"Very funny, smart ass. Now move so I can clean it up. Come on fool, m-m-ohhh," I moaned.

He was no longer putting kisses all over my ass cheeks. Now he had his tongue in my asshole and he was eating what he wanted for breakfast. It was a fast-paced game of tag between my pussy, my ass, and his tongue, but everybody was winning and I damn sure wasn't mad.

"W-wait, you gotta stop," I begged, even as I widened my stance to allow him more access to my beautiful butterfly. I could feel the hot grease popping up and hitting my titties, but the heat in between my legs was the center of my attention.

"Oh shit! Big, stop pl-playing! Ohhh shit!" I yelled, grabbing onto the counter as the clouds parted and the storm of my orgasm poured into his waiting mouth.

For a moment I barely knew where I was, but suddenly the smell of my food burning snapped me back to reality. I tried to finish what I'd started, but when I felt his dick poking at my dripping pussy, I knew he wanted to finish what he'd started. I opened my mouth to ask for just five minutes, but before I could get a word out I felt his hand around my throat and his dick plowing into me hard enough to have me on my tippy toes.

"Big!" I exclaimed, barely having time to switch the burners off before he spun me around and had me face down on my kitchen table.

The ride was rough because he was pounding me harder than any hurricane, but he knew how much I loved this shit.

"You love me?" he growled.

"Y-yes! Yesssss!" I screamed, cumming hard enough to bring tears of pure bliss to my eyes.

He came right behind me, intensifying my own orgasm more than I thought humanly possible. For several minutes we stayed in what probably looked like an awkward and uncomfortable position with me laying halfway across the table, while the back half of me was still in the air supported by his one arm and his dick.

"Bae, I-I still smell food burning," I panted, trying to catch my breath. When he finally let me touch the earth again and climbed out of me, I turned around to find a cloud of smoke hovering about us.

Apparently, I hadn't shut the stove off completely and now the smoke detector was screaming in protest. I wanted to smack the self-satisfied smirk off his face, but somehow, I knew it matched my own.

"Get the smoke detector," I said, pushing him playfully.

Moving fast despite my growing soreness, I grabbed the now-ruined pan of potatoes and threw them in the sink, turning the cold water on to counter the heat.

"You just gonna have to settle for bacon, eggs, and sausage because I ain't cutting up no more potatoes for you," I hollered over the still blaring smoke detector.

It was hard to believe I almost let a nigga burn my house down because I couldn't say no to his sex! In fairness though, Big wasn't just any nigga, and the sex was on another level that I couldn't describe with words. Damn, was this what being addicted felt like? Finally, the smoke detector went off and I could hear myself think again.

"You ain't finished cooking yet? I'm hungry as shit," Big said, coming back into the kitchen.

"Negro, please, it's your fault I ain't done and I'm standing here with cum running down my damn leg."

"Sorry, not sorry," he replied, slapping my ass before picking up all the stuff he'd knocked off the table and cleaning up the broken egg.

I finished up with the eggs, made our plates, and took them to the table.

"Come on, bae, you know I worked up a bigger appetite than this. Everything is bigger in Texas," he said, eyeing his plate of food.

"This is only a snack, babe. You know we got that fundraiser in a couple hours."

"Yea, but they don't be having no real food at them type of events and your man needs to eat," he replied, picking up his fork and doing just that.

"I'm still surprised you insisted on going with me. And don't think I ain't notice how you've been dicking me down all day to avoid telling me why you're really here."

"I told you, it's just business," he said vaguely around a mouthful of food.

"Regular business don't bring you and Rock down here unannounced," I replied, noticing the hesitation of his fork on the way to his mouth. I started eating my own food to give him time to gather his thoughts because by now he realized I wasn't letting this go.

"Since when did you start asking questions about business?" he asked.

"I'm not asking for specifics, but there's obviously a problem. I texted my dad and told him I was skipping school today, and do you know what he said? Nothing. I know I'm a grown woman in college, but for my father to not even ask why I wasn't in school means he's either too preoccupied to care, or he wants me with you. Which is it?"

"You too smart for your own good," he said, shaking his head.

"I'll take that as a compliment. Now start talking," I insisted.

"We came down for a meeting because there's some serious shit in the air, but that's really all I can tell you right now."

"That's all I need to know. I'm guessing you're gonna be stuck up my ass for a while, huh?"

"I didn't know you were ready to unlock that door, but I'm down if you are," he replied, smiling devilishly.

"You know what I mean, smart ass."

"Yeah, I'ma stay close until we go back to Houston and then - "

"Hold up, until who goes to Houston?" I asked quickly.

"Come on, bae, you know the base of operations is out there and I gotta make sure shit is running smoothly."

"And you know school is here, which makes this my base of operations. You can relocate. I can't," I stated logically.

For a moment he simply looked at me, and then he went back to the plate in front of him. One thing I loved about Big was that he knew when he couldn't win an argument with me, and unlike most dudes, he didn't just keep hammering away until he pissed me off. My man was smart.

"I'm 'bout to take a shower and get ready," I announced, getting up and putting my plate in the sink. "Oh, and you got the dishes since you made such a mess in the kitchen," I said over my shoulder as I walked out of the kitchen.

I could hear him mumbling something under his breath, but I couldn't make out the words. It didn't matter though because I knew my spot would be clean by the time I finished pampering myself. Once I had my outfit picked out and laid across my bed I turned in the direction of the bathroom, only to find Big standing in the bedroom doorway.

"No more sex right now. My pussy is sore enough," I said, half-jokingly.

I'd expected some type of smart-ass retort or at least a smirk, but he just stood there with the weirdest look on his face.

"Babe, what's wrong?" I asked, getting an uneasy feeling.

He still wasn't saying anything, but now he was moving towards me.

"Big, talk to me," I demanded.

"It's…it's your dad, bae."

Immediately I felt my heart hit the floor. The words I anticipated coming out of his mouth were words I'd dreaded since I was old enough to understand what it was my dad really did. I didn't want to hear them though.

"No, no, Big, no - "

"He's not dead, but…he's been kidnapped."

The feelings of relief and despair hit with such intensity that it caused me to go numb, and Big ended up carrying me to my bed, where he laid me down. For what seemed like an eternity I could only lay there and look at the ceiling in search of answers that didn't live up there.

"Wh-what happened?" I heard myself ask in a voice I didn't recognize.

"All Rock was able to tell me was that a meeting with the Sinaloa Cartel had gone bad, and sometime after that, word came through that they had Soloman."

"What about Jacob?" I asked, fighting the tears in my throat.

"He's fine, but I won't know more until we get to Houston. Rock and Ebony are already headed that way."

"I can't go to Houston."

"What?" he asked.

"I can't go to Houston. I've gotta go be with my mom," I said, getting up off the bed and hurrying into my closet to find something to throw on.

Sixty seconds later I was in jeans, a T-shirt, and some Air Max, headed for the door.

"Hold up a second. Damn, let me put some clothes on," Big hollered after me.

I heard him, but I kept it moving downstairs in search of my phone and keys. I found the phone, but it took a few minutes of searching before I remembered that EB had my fucking car.

"Big, come the fuck on!" I yelled, finally losing my battle with the tears now flowing freely from my eyes.

Thankfully he appeared within seconds, still half naked with only his jeans and boots on and his pistol in his hand.

With a T-shirt slung over his shoulder, he followed me out the door and we quickly hopped in the back of his truck, startling the sleeping driver.

"Nigga, wake up and get us to her parents' house ASAP," Big ordered, pulling out his phone and texting with lightning speed.

I couldn't stop my tears from flowing. All I could do was lay my head back against the seat and pray with my eyes closed. My father had never lied to me or my mother, so we understood the danger attached to his business. In theory. Nothing like this had ever happened before though, and for it to be someone he was in business with made it worse because they understood what he was capable of. That reality would make them less willing to let him live.

"How could this happen, Big? My father is careful. He's smart, and you know that," I said, fighting the urge to openly sob.

"I don't know, bae. I'm trying to find out everything I can right now. Trust me, I'ma get to the bottom of this shit, I promise."

I felt his hand reaching for mine and I grabbed it without hesitation, needing him to anchor me in this storm because my sanity was just about blown away.

After the longest thirty minutes of my life, we pulled up in front of my parents' house and I hopped out at a dead run towards the front door. Not having a house key didn't prevent me from getting in thanks to the palm scanner my dad had installed a while ago.

"Mom!" I yelled as soon as I crossed the threshold. I didn't get an immediate response, so I took the stairs two at a time, thinking she was probably in bed resting.

"Mom!" I called out again.

When I didn't find her in any of the rooms upstairs, my heart began beating wildly as thoughts of her being kidnapped too flooded my brain.

"Mom, where are you?" I yelled, coming back downstairs and heading for the kitchen.

Before I'd made it halfway down the hall I saw part of her foot sticking out, causing me to take off at dead sprint.

"Mom! Mommy! Bae, get in here!" I screamed hysterically, sliding to a stop next to her prone figure stretched out on the kitchen floor.

"Oh God, Mom, no!"

CHAPTER 6
SOLOMAN
One week later…

"Is it too much to ask to get some decent food?" I asked, staring at the plate in front of me.

"Sorry the accommodations aren't up to your usual standards, but I was always told that a hungry dog will eat anything."

"Yeah, and I thought all you cartel boys made serious money, but eating beans and rice every day makes you just like every other poor Mexican," I replied, smiling.

Of course, my comment cost me a thunderous left hook from the man standing beside me, and by the time my vision cleared, I could see the man in front of me smiling. Some would say it was foolish of me to antagonize my captor, but it had been my hope to force them into making a mistake. As long as it didn't kill me.

"Enjoy your delicious meal," the man in front of me said, nodding to his partner, who followed him out of the room.

I didn't know their names. Hell, I didn't even know what day it was. But I knew if I got out of this alive, I'd kill them both in the most gruesome way possible.

My first few days had been spent in a drug-induced fog, probably to make transporting me easier, and when I was finally allowed out of that fog, I was being guarded by these two idiots. To me, they obviously weren't bright or else they wouldn't have gone along with this whole thing, but they weren't exactly stupid either. Right now, I was kicking myself in the ass for never learning to speak Spanish like Ivy had encouraged because that's the only way they communicated amongst themselves.

I was kept in one room of the dingy, rundown apartment, and the only time I was allowed out was to cross the hall and use the bathroom. At first, I'd tried to learn everything I could about the layout of the place, but I quickly learned that all the windows were boarded up because it was always pitch black in the hallway. The light in my room was a single bulb kept on at all times, probably to prevent sleep. I didn't even know if I was still on U.S. soil, but every day a picture was taken for proof of life. I didn't know who the pictures were going to, especially since my best friend turned out to be a real-life Judas.

Ever since I'd been able to hold a clear thought in my head, I'd been trying to understand how the nigga I grew up with, the nigga the game had made my partner for life, could do this to me. It just didn't make sense. I mean, if he was having cold feet about our normal operations and wanted out, I would've willingly let him walk without any hard feelings. So why play his hand like this?

During the meeting he'd tried giving off the impression that it was just smart business, but the only conclusion I could come to was that he wanted it all to himself. The problem with that was that he didn't have what it would take to maintain control. Only a king could run a kingdom. As sick as I was of rice and beans, I still knew it was counterproductive to starve myself, so I choked the meal down as best I could. The fact that all I was given to drink was bottled water really made me believe I was in Mexico because not even the natives trusted their water to drink.

After finishing my meal, I stood up to prepare for my daily exercises, which helped to keep both my mind and body moving in the right direction. The door suddenly opened again. This time I knew exactly who the man was strolling through it though.

"I would ask how you're doing, but I think we're past false pleasures, amigo," José said, taking a seat at the one table in the room where I'd been sitting. My choices were to either sit on the makeshift cot I'd been given or sit across from him. I chose the latter so he'd understand I wouldn't cower before him.

"We're past you calling me amigo too, pussy," I said, taking a seat. I could feel the blow coming from behind, but he waved his man off and just smiled at me for a second.

"A lot of fight in you. I like that. It won't do you any good though, and I'd much rather we were friends than enemies," José said, pulling out a cigar and lighting it.

"You never struck me as dumb until all this shit happened, but now I know you must be absolutely stupid if you think we can be friends."

"You don't want to be my friend? That is upsetting, especially since I'm continuing to make you money while you're on vacation. You'll be happy to know that our first two runs have been successful and very lucrative for everyone involved. Estéban is pleased," he said, smiling.

Estéban was the head of the cartel and someone I'd once trusted. I didn't know if he knew the circumstances of this latest business venture, but I'd be sure to ask him personally if I got out this situation. "I would say congratulations, but we both know I don't mean it. What I really wanna know is how long you think this shit will last before the Port Authority gets wise to what's going on?" I asked, smiling now too.

"Ah, but that's the beauty. You see, border patrol and I.C.E. focus on the border and the wall your president keeps threatening to build, but we're sending our people to countries the U.S. considers allies and then bringing them in. Sort of like that Trojan horse thing you read about in history books. So even if a shipment of people does get caught, it won't be coming from Mexico, and it won't have the cartel's fingerprints on it," he concluded, giving me an even bigger self-satisfied grin.

I could admit that his plan wasn't as flawed as I'd expected, but I'd only admit that to myself. Outwardly I kept a neutral expression and continued staring at him.

"Despite your lack of enthusiasm, I know you're impressed. All you have to do is come on board and this uncomfortable situation ends."

"Come on board," I echoed, not changing my expression in the slightest.

"Yes, come on board. This idea and proposition was never formulated with the intent of you not being included - at least not from my perspective. I never thought you lacked vision, just the cojones to do things you find distasteful in the name of a greater good. But now that you know this business can be done with no more risk than you've already had in your life, it doesn't make sense for you not to come on board, amigo."

I evaluated him and his words silently. He probably thought I was giving the other cartel consideration, especially after all I'd been through, but I was thinking about what he didn't say with regards to Jacob. It was clear that he and my former partner had discussed things at great length and were of the same mind, even though Jacob thought he could do this deal without me. So what was keeping me alive? What had this man sitting across from me asking for my help?

"It seems like you and Jacob have things under control. You don't need my help," I said, knowing the opposite was true.

"You are right. We can do this just fine without you. With you on board though, we all can make ten times more money than we do now. Especially with your connections."

The last part of his statement was the real reason he was sitting across from me trying to play nice, and probably the reason I was alive altogether. They needed my connections because the people I had inside the two major port authorities in Texas were loyal to me, and the dummy corporations set up to funnel the money in the right direction for the Port Authority were in my name. Sure, shit was running smooth for them now, but it wouldn't be for long without my help.

"All money ain't good money, so thanks, but no thanks," I replied.

For a moment José didn't speak, but the frustration was easy to read in his dark brown eyes. He'd tried to convince me to join the money train by appealing to both my business sense and my greed by saying only what he wanted me to hear, but he'd forgotten how long I'd been doing this. A real boss listened to the silence closer than any words spoken.

"Have you not been through enough to know that you really don't have a choice, amigo? Or do you need to suffer more?" he asked, his threat undeniable despite his calm tone.

"In my fifty years there ain't been shit I ain't seen or done, so all that lolly-popping and threatening you're doing is pointless."

"Lolly-popping? I don't know what the means," he replied.

"That means running your dick suckers, as in those lips on your face. I ain't no bitch, so stop trying to play me like one," I advised.

This time he didn't stop the blow that landed squarely in the back of my head, causing my vision to swim, but the look of rising anger on his face was worth it.

"You gain nothing by pissing me off, Soloman. You only lose."

"And you gain nothing by holding me, so I guess we should just call this a draw and move the fuck on," I replied, still blinking rapidly in an effort to clear the double vision I was now experiencing.

"So far we have done things the easy way because you have some good business with us. Make no mistake about who we are, and what we'll do to that pretty wife and daughter you cherish to get what we want," he stated calmly.

It took every ounce of restraint in my body not to leap across the table and snap this mu'fucka's neck, and the only thing preventing it was the knowledge that the threat would be carried out even swifter if I killed him. The rage I was feeling coursing through my veins literally made my body feel like it was on fire from the inside out. Still, I knew I only had one play I could make in this situation, and so with great effort I let all emotion dry up until I was blizzard cold inside.

"Had you been anyone else I might've laughed your threats off, but I know all too well that you and your associates will make good on what you say. The problem is that you're coming at me like some ordinary nickel and dime type street nigga. I'm not a thug or a hooligan hustling for sneaker money, and I damn sure don't pass my time with this street life. I'm the truth. I'm a businessman. More importantly than that, I'm a mu'fuckin' gangsta who knows that the boogie man is real because I break bread with him over the body of a mu'fucka like you. Do you think I don't have an insurance plan? A little leverage? And protection for my family? My suggestion is that you go speak with Estéban before you threaten my family again. And while you're at it, you might wanna check on those you love too," I said, winking and leaning back in the chair to study him as closely as he was me.

José and I weren't strangers, obviously, because we got to the money together, but he wasn't up close and personally familiar with how I handled my enemies. He was smart enough to surmise that I hadn't achieved my success by being anything less than ruthless, and I could tell that by the way he was now evaluating me. Had I shown even the slightest hint of weakness, he would've smelled victory like wild animals do fear. Now he wasn't as sure of himself because he knew that I knew he was a killer, and the cartels notoriously killed without remorse. So did I.

"You talk tough, but there are things worse than death, amigo. I know how much you love your family and what it would do to you to watch them mutilated before your very eyes. You should think about that," he said, standing up.

"I don't need to think about shit - "

This time I didn't anticipate the blow coming, and it was delivered with enough force to push me face first onto the table. Briefly I saw José smiling down at me. And then I saw nothing.

CHAPTER 7
EBONY

"Damn, you've been looking at that same blank screen for over an hour now. Give it up, bae."

"Well if I didn't have you sitting in the corner watching my every move, maybe I could get some shit done. I mean, we're in arguably the safest place right now, Rock, so why are you hovering?" I asked, clearly annoyed.

"Didn't know I was bothering you, but I can find something else to do," he replied, getting up from his spot on my bed and walking out the door.

I hadn't meant to hurt his feelings, but being cooped up in my parents' house under their constant supervision, and his, was enough to make me reconsider boarding school. I wasn't stupid. I understood that my father and my uncle Sol were at war. But I hated how it was affecting my life too. Not only was I forced to take all of my classes online to avoid failing the semester, I couldn't even hang out or see any of my friends! I couldn't see my best friend. That was killing me the most because I knew Ivy needed me right now, but we hadn't spoken in a week and I couldn't understand why.

Text after text I'd sent, begging her to leave the hospital for a little while and come spend time with us, if only to give her mind a rest, but I got no response. I had absolutely no idea how she was holding up after not only the kidnapping, but her mom's heart attack on top of everything. All I knew was that she was my sister and we needed each other right now more than ever.

After another five minutes of staring at the flashing cursor waiting on me to begin typing my economics paper, I finally did as Rock suggested and gave up. Shutting my laptop down,

I left my bedroom and followed my nose to the kitchen, where I found my mother hard at work.

"Hi, Mommy," I said, taking a deep breath as I climbed up on the stool across from her.

"Hi, baby. I'd ask you what's wrong, but the cloud of smoke and flying gravel your boyfriend left suggests a little bit of everything. Don't worry. I'm making your favorite comfort food."

"Gumbo?" I asked, closing my eyes and inhaling the aroma deeply.

"Indeed it is. Now, tell me what's wrong."

"Aw, Mom, you're right. It's everything. I'm not really mad at Rock. It's just that I've been stuck in this damn house for a week and he's not giving me any breathing room."

"Truth be told, there ain't that much breathing room for any of us, despite how big this house is. Your father has us locked up nice and tight and trust me, I'm starting to get cabin fever my damn self," she replied, stirring the delicious-smelling food slowly, staring into it the way a fortune teller would a crystal ball.

"But why, Mom? I mean, he and Uncle Sol have had to go through some rough shit before, but - "

"But this is different. Soloman was taken, and the only person who can secure his return is your father. That has put immense pressure on him, not just for our sake and protection, but for Ivy and Margarita as well."

"Do you know how Aunt Rita is doing?" I asked.

"All I know is that they were able to save her life after the heart attack, but she slipped into a coma."

Suddenly the tasty-smelling food wasn't holding the same appeal, but I managed to hold down the bile along with my deepening sadness.

"You haven't spoken to Ivy?" my mom asked, her words tinged with the same disbelief I felt.

"No. She's not answering her phone or any of my text messages."

"Well, you know it's against hospital policy to have phones in patient rooms, so - "

The look I gave her forced her to leave the hollow excuses floating in the wind because we both knew that if Ivy wasn't responding, it was because she didn't want to.

"Just give her time, Ebony. She'll come around, and when she does, she's gonna need your love and support."

"I know. So, is Dad gonna be home for dinner?" I asked, changing the subject.

"Who knows? He's the only one that gets to come and go as he pleases around here anymore."

I could hear the anger in her tone, which was a warning to tread lightly with this particular subject.

"Where is he exactly?" I asked.

"Somewhere out of the country, but he's due back between today and tomorrow. Honestly, I'm not cooking for him. This is for us girls," she said, reaching across the breakfast bar and giving my hand a firm squeeze.

One thing I'd learned about my mother is that no matter what was going on, she knew a way to make it alright for me, and I loved her for that.

"Can I ask you a question, Mom, kind of a personal one?"

"Of course you can, sweetheart. Talk to me."

"You're a strong woman, a strong, independent woman with her own money, and you were raised a certain way. So why is Dad's lifestyle acceptable to you?" I asked, truly curious.

I could tell by the look on her face that this wasn't the question she'd expected, and for a moment she was closed off to me as the shadow of something long forgotten passed over her.

"Why do you accept Rock's lifestyle? Because you love him. Well, I love your father, but even more than that, I understand that men like him have a place in this world, a necessary place. Once upon a time, all the money in the world couldn't fix what was wrong with my life. Your father did though, and because of that, I love him and accept whatever he has to do in the name of survival today. It's that simple."

I'd never asked her this question, although it had crossed my mind over the years. Hearing her answer made me understand why being with Rockafella didn't bother me, even though I knew what he did. Some would call men like him and my father evil, but they were necessary evils, and I would go to my grave believing that.

"How long do we got before dinner is done?" I asked.

"About fifteen minutes. You've got time to make up with your man, but he's still not invited to dinner. I just want to eat with you."

Any other time her comment might've inspired an argument, but I knew she wasn't saying it because she disliked Rock. She just wanted to comfort me and give me the girl bond I was missing without my sister Ivy. Hopping off the stool, I came around the counter and gave her a quick kiss on the cheek before heading back upstairs. I'd left my phone next to my laptop on my desk, and when I got to it, I was pleasantly surprised with a waiting message from the devil himself.

"Sorry about storming out. I know you're not really mad at me and I love you enough to give you some space. I'll be back soon," I read aloud from the text message.

My response was the emoji smiley face that had hearts for eyes, and I sent him a pair of lips too. I loved having an understanding man because I was nothing if not difficult sometimes, and arguing with that nigga wasn't always a bad thing because the sex was crazy afterwards! We'd have to keep it rated mature while I was under my parents' roof because the last thing I wanted my mom or dad to hear was me acting a fool on the dick. That wouldn't be cute. The good thing was that I knew just what to do to inspire my man to make every moment and thrust inside me count.

Scrolling through the settings on my phone, I selected what I needed and then propped my phone up next to my laptop before backing up slowly. Quietly I began a seductive striptease, swaying my hips to music only I could hear while pulling my T-shirt over my head. I knew the suspense would be immediate because I didn't have a bra on and my nipples were hard enough to cut glass. Still I took my time, licking first one finger and rubbing a nipple and then repeating the gesture with the other sensitive gumdrop. Even while doing this, my hips continued to roll slowly, reminiscent of a Jamaican dirty wind, as I slowly pushed my sweatpants and panties to the floor. Once they'd reached their destination, I stepped out of them, taking a seat on the bed behind me and spreading my legs until my beautifully-trimmed pussy was winking at the camera.

All I was wearing was my socks and a smile, and the thought of what would be done to me later from this video made me smile wider. It also made my pussy throb harder. Making steady eye contact with my phone, I put my left leg up on my bed and used my left hand to go under it to get to my pussy lips. After pushing two fingers inside myself slowly and deliberately, I pulled them out before guiding my hand to my mouth and sucking my juices off with a loud slurp. I repeated the process two more times, damn near pushing myself to the point where I was gonna have to finish myself off, when I heard my mother calling for me.

Reluctantly, I climbed off the bed and walked back over to my desk, picking up my phone and blowing my man one final kiss before ending the recording. I didn't even bother watching it for fear that I'd become even more aroused and forced to miss dinner, but I sent it to Rock with a message to hurry home. After washing my hands, I quickly threw my clothes back on and was headed out of my bedroom door when I heard my phone vibrating on my desk. Anticipating a message from Rock and a dick picture I hurried to it, but what I found instead was a complete shock. Ivy had finally broken the silence with a simple text instructing me to call her. Without hesitation I hit her number, needing to hear my sister's voice in the worst way. After four rings the phone was answered with silence.

"Damn, bitch, it took you long enough to get back to me. I've been worried sick!" I said, happy despite all that had happened because I'd missed her that much.

"I ain't have shit to say. I still don't. What do you want, Ebony?"

"E-excuse me?" I replied, happiness quickly transforming into disbelief at both her words and the coldness with which she spoke.

"What – do – you – want?" she asked again, in the same tone.

"I wanted to know what was going on with my aunt, and to make sure you were okay, but right now I wanna know why you're talking to me like some random bitch."

For endless seconds loud silence was what I got in response, almost to the point that I'd thought she hung up. Then I heard her take a deep breath, along with the familiar sound of metal grinding against metal swiftly, but I couldn't place the sound to know what she was doing.

"Ivy, talk to me. I know this shit ain't easy, sis, and I feel your pain, so - "

"Bitch, you don't know my pain," she growled.

We called each other "bitch" all the time in an endearing way, but there was no love in the use of the word in this moment. Part of me wanted to bite back, but I realized she was telling the truth.

"You're right, I don't know your pain, and for the first time in our lives, you won't let me in. I love your parents as if they were my own, and you know that. We're family, Ivy, and you don't have to go through any of this heartache alone. I'm here for you," I declared emotionally, fighting the tears streaming down my face.

It was clear to me that my sister was hurting beyond anything I could imagine, but all I could do right now was convince her that I would be here for her no matter what.

"Ivy?" I called out after another deafening silence from her end of the phone.

"I'm only telling you this because of all that we've been through, so listen closely because I'm not repeating myself. We ain't family. Once upon a time we were, but those days are over - "

"What the fuck are you talking 'bout? Look, I know you're going through a lot and you're scared, but don't push me away!" I said, fighting now to keep my anger I check.

"You heard what I said. My advice is that you stay in Houston where it's safe."

"W-wait a minute, hold the fuck up! Bitch, are you threatening me?" I asked in utter disbelief.

This was my best friend on the other end of this phone, my sister in every way that mattered. Surely she wasn't on no bullshit like this.

"I'm simply telling you it's a war going on and no one is safe. Not even your father."

I opened my mouth to ask her what the fuck that meant, but there was no doubt that I'd be talking to myself. Ivy was gone, and not just off the phone. From the way the conversation went, she was out of my life for good. Like a bolt of lightning, a realization came to me that left me with a chill that radiated from head to toe. The noise that I'd heard in the background went from feeling familiar to being completely recognizable. It was the sound of a bullet being chambered in a pistol. It was the sound of death.

CHAPTER 8
JACOB

"Go – go – go –slower," I instructed breathlessly, wrapping my right hand in the long raven mane of the Spanish beauty kneeling before me.

My left hand was behind me on the bed, keeping me in a semi-sitting position while I watched in delighted fascination as the woman gobbled my dick. If it weren't for the tears in her eyes, I would've sworn she loved how my dick threatened to destroy her vocal cords with each downward bob of her head.

Deep down I knew she probably hated me as much as what she was doing to me, but I couldn't let that affect whether I enjoyed this or not. The short Mexican holding the AK-47 standing by the door would undoubtedly report back to José if I faked it, and José was not the type to trust a man who couldn't enjoy getting his dick sucked. No matter the circumstances.

"That – that's it," I said once she found a steady rhythm that didn't make her gag and still allowed me maximum pleasure.

Within minutes my vision blurred, and I saw the gorgeous woman demolishing my dick through the eyes of intense orgasmic pleasure. Unintentionally I held her head in place as my seed poured into her mouth, but after a moment it became too much for her and she pulled back violently before bolting for the bathroom. Before she'd taken five good steps, the little Mexican was on her, catching her flush in the stomach with the butt of the assault rifle, causing her to double over and spit cum all over the cheap brown carpet.

Given the shitty state of the motel we were in somewhere in Tijuana, it was a safe bet that this carpet had seen its fair share of semen. Still, I felt bad for the woman now cowering beneath the boots of the angry Mexican as the blows and insults rained on her. I was smart enough to keep my sympathy to myself though, and instead I focused on cleaning myself up. By the time I'd finished cleaning myself, the ass kicking was over, the girl was permitted into the bathroom, and the little Mexican was back in his original position like nothing had happened. All I could do was keep sitting on the bed with my poker face intact, thankful that this was the last girl to entertain. I'd spent the weekend hopping from motel to motel, from pussy to mouth to ass, and in some cases, all three with two women at the same damn time!

While some men might consider that heaven, I would argue that it can only be heaven if that's what you want. Otherwise, it's just a lot of work. José had been adamant that I sample thirteen of the best women he was sending across the border in our next shipment, and adamant was an understatement. What he didn't say was that I was still proving that I was completely okay with our new business arrangement.

To be honest, the business didn't bother me because I didn't give a fuck who he shipped or what their purpose was, just as long as it turned a profit. What I wasn't okay with was cheating on my wife, especially when I know in any other situation I would've needed to see some of those girls' I.D.'s for age verification. I wasn't exactly doing business with the moral police though, and none of their lives were worth mine.

My thoughts were interrupted by the woman coming out of the bathroom and resuming her position in front of me.

"I – I'm sorry. I will swallow," she vowed, reaching for the zipper to my slacks with shaking hands.

"It's okay," I said, gently pushing her hands away. The sound of the slide being pulled on the AK signaling the first bullet's willingness to party caused her to flinch, and my eyes to snap to those of the glaring Mexican.

"I have a prior engagement and José knows about it," I said, tapping my watch face.

Without a word, and with a firm grip on his weapon, he pulled out his phone and quickly tapped out a message. Again, the woman in front of me reached for my zipper, her eyes full of silent pleas, but I took her hands in mine and shook my head. A minute later the man got a message back that made him quickly open the door, and in walked José with two more armed men trailing him.

"Buenos tardes, amigo. I trust Irena treated you well," he said.

"Better than I'd hoped. I wouldn't mind going another round, but you know I have a meeting in the States that I must get to."

"Can it not be put off? I'm sure Irena would like to spend more time with you," he said, moving closer until he could reach down and pet her head as if she were a Doberman.

"You of all people know the importance of this meeting if I am to gain control of the Galveston and Laredo ports."

"If you are to gain control?" he asked quickly.

"If we are to gain control," I replied, releasing Irena's hands and standing up.

For a moment we simply stood there staring at each other, nothing between us except a silence that was heating up, and a terrified Irena. Finally, José's facial features relaxed a little bit and the building tension was avoided, for the moment.

"Allow me to escort you to the airfield," José offered, stepping aside and allowing me to move freely out of the room.

The two men that had been standing behind José led the way downstairs and into the alley, where three black

Expeditions waited. José and I quickly ducked into the middle truck and moments later we were whisked through the side streets and back alleys.

"So, what do you think of our product?" José asked, lighting a cigar.

"Muy bueno. Wherever you set up shop with them, you're guaranteed to make money."

"We're guaranteed to make money, amigo. That's what I'm trying to get you to see. The drugs are a good business, along with extortion and other things. But the pussy is the oldest business, and it will sell even in a drought," he replied, smiling wickedly.

Even if I didn't agree with his tactics, I had to agree with his logic. Sex would sell long after my black ass was dead and gone from this world, and just like every other scheme, it was as American as apple pie. No reason not to profit.

"When do you want to send them?" I asked.

"That's the attitude I like to see from my business partner. Eager to get to the money…or maybe the merchandise," he said, laughing.

"The money always comes first."

"Sí. And with that in mind, I think we should move within the next seventy-two hours if you have no objections, or other business matters that are more important."

"My primary focus is today's meeting because that affects all business. After that, it should be smooth sailing," I replied.

"And how confident are you in winning over the trust of those Soloman has in his very deep pockets?" José asked, all signs of jokes and laughter completely evaporating from the conversation.

I knew this talk was the real reason he offered to escort me to the private airfield where my plane was stashed. There was no doubt in my mind that it would take longer than a week to break Soloman, if he could be broken at all. Just as surely as I knew that, I knew that the cartel wasn't known for its patience either, and that's why I had another plan.

"I believe I can convince all parties involved that it's in everyone's best interest to keep making money. Everybody got bills to pay," I reasoned.

"True enough, but not everyone's loyalty can be bought," he replied, blowing a cloud of smoke in my face.

It was extremely hard resisting the temptation to send José's brains out the window behind him for his disrespect, but killing him meant certain death for me, so I bit my tongue.

"I'll handle my business, don't worry," I said, turning to look out my window in hopes of regrouping before shit went all bad.

"I believe that, amigo, because if you don't..."

The obvious threat hung in the air thicker than his cigar smoke, but still I didn't take the bait.

"I've already come up with another plan, since you can't seem to break Soloman," I said, feeling him bristle at the intended jab without having to look at him. Two could play the petty game.

"I'm listening," he said slowly.

"I know who controls everything in the event that Soloman dies or simply never returns."

"That would be his wife I'm sure, but - "

"But his wife is in a coma, so that means their daughter is in charge because she's the only heir to the throne," I said, finally looking at him.

"And you're willing to harm her should it come to this?"

"She's a spoiled little rich girl that calls me uncle. Knowing that I've always been her father's right hand, I'm naturally who she'll turn to when it comes to all the business affairs. I told you I got this," I stated confidently.

We spent the remainder of the ride in equal silence, both traveling with our thoughts on what the future night look like.

"Update me as soon as possible," he requested as I climbed out of the truck and headed towards my plane.

I didn't give him a backwards glance, let alone respond to what he'd said. At the present moment I was actually second guessing my decision to work with him instead of just going straight to Estéban. Hindsight was definitely 20/20, but the evil you know is always better than the one you don't. I quickly boarded my G-III and set about sending messages to confirm my meeting within the hour while my pilot did his preflight check.

On most occasions I preferred to drive into Mexico because it costs serious money to land on U.S. soil without a flight plan, especially in this day and age. Today I was glad to have chosen this method of transportation because I needed to get back home in a hurry. Ten minutes later I was airborne and feeling more relaxed than I had in the past two days, despite the stress-relieving activities I'd engaged in. I was actually anxious to get this business concluded so I could get home to my wife and make love to her tenderly.

In no way would that absolve the guilt, but it would go a long way towards us reconnecting and smoothing out the rough spots that came with me putting business first. Once the plane leveled off, and the meeting was confirmed, I sent Marissa a text that I would be home later tonight. I probably could've made it earlier, but I needed to stop and get her some sort of present as a peace offering first. Rule #1 as a husband was that when you fuck up, you make up, in any way you can.

An hour and a half later, I was stepping from the back of my 2017 gunmetal gray Escalade at the Laredo Port Authority, game face on and ready to conquer the business I'd helped build.

"Gentlemen, I apologize for being late. You know how international travel can get," I said, walking into the office and addressing the three white men seated at the conference table.

No one stood at my arrival, but I didn't take this as a personal affront. Unlike the office space we kept in Galveston, this office was built for comfort and represented our stature. The conference table was hand-carved walnut with matching colored plush leather swivel chairs surrounding it. The floors were a glossy hardwood about two shades darker than the table, with a gold trim bordering the walls. All the details were done in a gold color scheme to give the room a tasteful elegance, and I'd chosen to have the meeting here to symbolize our rise from the trenches.

"As each of you know this is a trying time, both in business and in our personal lives with the kidnapping of my brother," I said, taking a seat at the head of the table. "At the same time, you know like I do that Soloman would want us to do all we could to make sure everything we have is maintained, and money is coming in."

"We're very busy, Jacob, so please spare us the sales pitch," Louis said, leaning back in his chair.

Louis and Roger Jones were brothers, which was obvious by the similar athletic builds and clear blue eyes, with the only difference being their differing blond and brown hair colors. They looked alike and they thought alike, which is why the bored expression on Roger's face that matched Louis's words didn't surprise me. The Jones brothers ran the corporation that handled 90% of all business we conducted through the ports, which meant they had a vested interest in keeping shit moving. The problem for me was that they were used to dealing with

Soloman, and if that wasn't enough of an obstacle, the third part to this equation could certainly be.

Jeremy was the wild card because he actually worked for the Port Authority, and he had juice with ports around the world. Behind his slim bifocals and underneath that brown mop of hair lived a mind full of secrets and secret passageways. He never really said what he was thinking, at least not to me, so I wasn't quite sure what approach would work best on him. When in doubt, though, I had to go with greed.

"The bottom line is that if we want to see Soloman again, we've gotta do shit the way the cartel wants it done, and if we wanna grow this empire, we need to embrace the new business just as we did the old," I said.

"But how would Soloman feel about this new business?" Roger asked.

"Soloman was about making money. Business was never personal with him," I lied.

"Still, human trafficking is a risky endeavor," Jeremy chimed in.

"Look, as long as I'm in charge the risk is mine, and - "

"Who said you were in charge?" Louis asked, smirking.

"What the fuck do you mean? Soloman and I built this shit," I replied testily.

"True enough, but we've dealt exclusively with Soloman, and in his absence, we were instructed to deal with the next in line," Roger said.

"I am the next in line - or have you not been fucking listening?" I asked, my voice rising in anger at being challenged by these talking suits in front of me.

"Actually, I'm next in line," a voice said from behind me.

In my anger I hadn't noticed the bathroom door opening, nor had I heard it, but I didn't need to turn around to know who the voice belonged to. My surprise quickly turned into shock when I felt cold steel being pressed to my temple.

"Ivy, what – what the fuck are you doing?" I asked, tasting fear invade my mouth with every breath taken.

"Isn't it obvious, Uncle Jacob? I'm joining the family business. My first act is getting rid of you."

CHAPTER 9
IVY

"Any change, babe?" Big asked, creeping into my mom's hospital room behind me.

I shook my head no, unwilling to let go of her hand or look away from her face. She looked so peaceful, like she was sleeping a lazy winter afternoon away instead of fighting for her life somewhere beyond her subconscious. Aside from the involuntary eye flicker and occasional hand twitch, she hadn't moved in a week - at least, I thought it was a week. Shit, it felt like a century had passed since I found her collapsed on the kitchen floor.

Seeing her lying there like that had ripped my heart from my chest, and honestly, I had no idea even now how I'd managed to keep going. I had no idea if I'd ever see my father again, and with each beep from the machines providing my mom with life, I felt like she was slipping further away. Did she know my father was dead and wanted to be with him on the other side? Could I begrudge her that? What would I do in this world if I lost them both? It seemed like the questions navigating the highway of my mind were endless and there was no off ramp in sight.

"You need some rest, babe," Big said, putting a hand on my shoulder.

Again, I just shook my head, refusing to be anywhere except right by my mother's side where I was needed. Thankfully, the hospital hadn't objected to my around-the-clock presence, and they had actually been accommodating by providing me with blankets and a pillow so I could nap on the couch next to her bed. I couldn't remember the last time I'd actually slept, but right now I was thanking God for all those late night cram sessions that only left me a couple hours of rest before class. I knew I needed real sleep, along with real food and a bath, but what I needed even more than that was my mother. To lose her could be to lose myself in a way I could never prepare for.

"Sweetheart, you need - "

"What I need is for you not to push me on this, because we both know you won't win this argument," I said, trying to keep my frustration in check.

Big meant well, but it was time to leave well enough alone. I expected another attempt at convincing me to do the right thing, but instead, he put his phone in front of me so I could read the message he had pulled up. I read it once, and then again before turning my quizzical gaze on him.

"Why do my father's business associates need to talk to me?" I asked.

"Babe, if I knew the answer to that, I would've taken care of it myself."

"Well, how do I even know these mu'fuckas are for real? Look, I ain't got time for - "

"You're gonna make time, because they're definitely for real. And those ain't some street level dudes. This is the upper echelon, the inner sanctuary of your dad's operations. If they need to speak with you, there's a damn good reason," he said with unflinching seriousness.

Since he was still holding the phone in my face, I again read the message of condolence and the request to speak with me A.S.A.P. about an urgent matter. I had no idea who Roger, Louis, and Jeremy were, but Big had me thinking they were kind of a huge deal.

"Whatever it is, they can deal with Jacob. Wait, why didn't they already go to Jacob?" I asked.

"Now you're wondering the same shit I am."

"Did you ask Rockafella?" I asked, letting go of my mom's hand to take the phone from him.

"You know Rock is in Houston worried about Ebony and them. Plus, I figured if they didn't go to Jacob, then they didn't holla at Rock either. For whatever reason, they wanna talk to you."

Despite reading the message again, none of this shit made sense, but there was really no reason for it to considering that I wasn't a part of that world. I would have to trust Big's judgment on this. Besides, they might know something important that could lead to my dad.

"Sit with her," I instructed, getting up and walking out of the room.

On impulse, I started to call Ebony to see if she knew anything about these dudes, but I still wasn't ready to talk to her just yet. I wasn't angry at her, but I was scared that the jealousy I felt about her father not being kidnapped would come out and possibly destroy our relationship. EB was my bitch and I didn't wanna lose that over misplaced emotions.

I took the elevator down to the emergency intake area and then proceeded outside. It wasn't clear to me how I should approach this conversation, but my dad always said you learned more by listening then you did talking. With a couple taps on the phone's screen, the number that sent the text was ringing.

"Ms. Black?" a male voice answered on the second ring.

"Yes," I replied confidently.

"My name is Louis Jones and I work for you father. Before we go any further, I want you to know that I'm sorry for all you've had to endure, and also, this call is taking place on an encrypted line, so we can speak freely."

The fact that someone could be listening never crossed my mind, which was a testament to how green I was. I wasn't about to let Louis know this though.

"I appreciate the condolences, Mr. Jones, and since you can understand these extremely hard times, would you mind telling me what's so important that it couldn't wait?"

"As I said I, my brother, and Jeremy work for your father, and we have for years. I know you have no knowledge of what our business encompasses exactly, but you do know your father to be a man of thought before action. It is for this reason that I'm contacting you."

"Okay," I replied, still lost as to what this was about.

"I don't know if you know the details surrounding this kidnapping, but I'll tell you what I know. The Sinaloa Cartel has been one of your father's business partners and primary supplier for narcotics for a while now. In the last few years, they have been asking both him and Jacob to start bringing people into the country as well as the usual shipments of merchandise, but your father was against that. His morals wouldn't let him become involved in human trafficking. At his last meeting with the cartel, their asking became insisting. Since your father's disappearance, Jacob has been moving people like pieces on a chessboard, and that's not a coincidence. I think - we think - that Jacob went along with the deal with the long-term objective of taking complete control of what he and your father built.

"If neither Jacob nor Soloman agreed to what the cartel wants, they could kill them, but then they'd lose way too much money, which shifts the balance of power in their ongoing war. So it stands to reason that a united front between Jacob and Soloman is the only way to protect everybody. Why did Jacob side with the cartel?"

For a few moments his question just hung in the air as I tried making sense of everything I'd just heard. I'd had questions from the beginning, but I chalked it up to jealousy and frustration because I knew how much Jacob loved my father and us. On top of that, my primary focus had been my mother. Now those questions were resurfacing, and I didn't like the way they made me feel.

"So why are you bringing this to me, especially considering that Jacob is now your boss?" I asked.

"Because he's not our boss. We work for your father, and in his absence, we work for you."

"Me? I'm not in the game. I'm a college student, and - "

"With all due respect, Ms. Black, you're Soloman's daughter, and we were assured that if the need ever arose, you were who we should turn to."

"Assured? By who?" I asked, dumbfounded.

"Your father, of course. As I said before, he's a man of thought and careful planning. You may not be a part of the game, but you're intelligent, and your father believed in you."

His statements put me at a loss for words. It wasn't that I doubted whether he was being truthful, but I was never groomed to take over the family business. There's a huge difference between knowing what a stove is for, and actually cooking on the mu'fucka. What he was suggesting was insane!

"Listen, Mr. Jones, I don't know what you think I can do for you or anyone else. I've got a mother in a coma and - "

"And that makes you both of your parents' sole power of attorney. Trust me when I tell you that secret won't stay buried long, especially because Jacob is gonna need your help and approval to keep shit running smoothly. I know you wanna focus on your mom, but the reality is that your dad is still missing and there's a war going on that could be closer to home than anyone realizes," he said sincerely.

My brain felt like it would overload if I tried to process any more info, so I did the only sane thing left to do.

"I'll call you back," I said, hanging up before he could respond, and heading back inside the hospital.

During the elevator ride back to my mom's room, all I could ask myself was what the fuck was going on,

"We've gotta go," I said, coming through the door and quickly crossing the room to my mom's bedside.

I could see the look of complete confusion on Big's face as I gave my mom a kiss and squeezed her hand, but I simply motioned him to follow me.

"What's up?" he asked once we were in the elevator.

"I'll explain once we're in the truck."

I tried using the ride down to the underground garage to organize my thoughts, but this shit was too unreal to make sense. It was also too logical to deny.

"Babe, what's going on?" Big asked impatiently.

"I don't wanna have this discussion until we're on the move," I replied, stepping out of the elevator and looking around like I expected the cartel to be waiting on me.

Given how much time we'd been spending at the hospital, Big had sent his homies to a hotel, which meant it was just us in the truck and I could talk freely. Once we were locked inside and headed towards my parents' house, I ran down my whole conversation with Louis Jones. At the end of it all, I turned to gauge Big's expression and saw that it was screwed up like what the fuck?

"You look exactly how I feel," I said, shaking my head.

"This shit is just too crazy!"

"So you think he's lying?" I asked.

"Nah, I didn't say that. Actually, I don't think he would've come at you with no bullshit like this without being damn certain of himself. The question now is, what are you gonna do?"

"I have no fucking idea! You know my dad kept me far away from any of this shit, so I wouldn't know the first thing about running a criminal enterprise," I replied honestly.

"Well, the first thing you have to know is that it's not your enterprise to run until you take control of it, which means dealing with Jacob. Before we get to that, though, you need to stop doubting yourself because you're nowhere near as green as you claim, babe. You know how to handle a gun, and you've got good business sense."

"And? What the fuck does that mean?" I asked, becoming more frustrated.

"The two most important things you need in this game are that killer instinct to take what's yours, and the good sense to know how to keep it out of the law's hands. Whether you grew up in this business or not, you still have that strong foundation, just like Michael Corleone in *The Godfather*."

Most females my age probably would've given him a blank stare at *The Godfather* reference, but because of Big's love for old gangster movies, I knew exactly what he meant. The question I had for myself was this: could I really do all that needed to be done? The remainder of the ride to my parents' house was spent in silence while I analyzed that question from every angle, knowing that I would need unshakeable confidence and 100% conviction to pull this off.

"I need you to give me a crash course in all the things I need to know," I said once we'd pulled up in front of the house.

"I got you," Big replied.

As soon as we got inside, I made a pot of coffee and we set up shop in my father's home office. For the next four hours Big took me from the streets, where metric tons of dope were broken down and sold, up through the legal businesses like tax returns. Sometimes I felt like my brain would simply shut down from all the info I was trying to store in it, but I was fueled by determination born of my father's belief in me. Even though I knew how to handle a gun, part of my new education was to learn how to break them down, clean them, and reassemble them.

"I feel like Forest Gump," I said, oiling the barrel of my dad's AR-15.

"More like Bubba because your ass move slow as hell!" he replied, laughing.

"Fuck you, punk! You over there cleaning a .38 and shit."

"I'ma tackle this ooh whop next. I didn't even know your pops was strapped like this. I mean, this nigga got Uzis, grenades, and probably more shit you just ain't pulled out yet," he said, looking around the room at the firepower I'd pulled out of the safe.

Even though I was kept far away from the street, my dad made sure that survival wasn't a secret I had to learn the hard way. There was actually very little my dad kept from me, and knowing this brought a nagging question to my mind.

"Be quiet for a minute," I said, setting the gun down and pulling my phone out.

"What are you doing?"

"Ebony is as close to her dad as I am to mine, so I wanna check this bitch's temperature," I said, sending her a text.

Moments later my phone rang and I answered it. The whole time we spoke I kept my eyes glued to Big, fighting to keep my cool while this bitch was going through her act of being concerned. Maybe she was, but sometime in the last few hours I'd come to understand what had to be done. Part of me knew that I owed her the benefit of doubt because of all that we meant to each other, but paranoia had me seeing things clearer. Maybe she did love my parents and maybe she was concerned about everything that was going on, but if she had to choose between my family and hers, who would she choose? I knew who I would choose. It was time to show that blood was thicker than water. Once the call was over, I got back to cleaning the guns, needing to keep my hands busy so I didn't have to see them shaking.

"You alright?" Big asked softly.

"No, but I know it's only gonna get worse before it gets better."

"What do you need me to do?" he asked sincerely.

I let his question hang in the air like the smell of gun oil while I put the AR-15 back together.

"I need to know that I can trust you. Always," I said, locking eyes with him while jamming the clip into the assault rifle and pulling the slide back.

"Always," he repeated, gaze unwavering.

With that conversation out of the way, I turned back to my phone and redialed a number from earlier.

"Ms. Black?" a familiar voice answered immediately.

"What is it you want me to do, Mr. Jones?" I asked.

"Attend a meeting that Jacob called us to at the Laredo Port Authority office in a few hours. Maybe then we can all get the answers we need."

"Send the location to my phone. I'll be there," I promised, disconnecting the call.

"Be where?" Big asked.

"Some meeting in Laredo between my father's associates and Jacob."

"You sure about this?" he asked, carefully examining my face.

"Do you think it's a trap?"

"No, but I think there's only one way this goes, and I'm not sure how you'll feel if I kill Jacob," he replied.

"Don't worry, you're not gonna kill him. We need to leave within the next thirty minutes," I said, leaving him sitting where he was while I went to take a quick shower and make myself presentable.

Twenty minutes later I was back, feeling revived in my little black dress and matching clutch.

"Damn! Why you look so good?"

"Stay focused, babe, and hand me that nickel-plated .45 in front of you," I said, holding my hand out. Once I had it tucked securely in my purse, I was ready for action.

"You ready?" I asked.

"Yeah, my niggas are out front."

"Well, send them back to the hotel because it's just us," I replied, turning and walking out of the room before he could argue.

When I got outside I signaled for his cousin to get out of the driver seat of Big's truck and I took his place behind the wheel. While Big explained what was going on, I punched the meeting location into the GPS and found the quickest route to take.

"We've got three hours to get there," I said once Big was in the passenger seat with the door closed.

You're running the show," he replied with a smile.

I couldn't deny that I liked the sound of that and I let it run through my head like a mantra during the drive to Laredo. Two and a half hours later, though, I was sitting down with my father's business associates, wondering what the hell I was doing.

"I like that you came alone," Jeremy said.

"My man is outside," I replied confidently.

"Oh, we're familiar with Big Cuzz, but you coming alone shows that you not only believe us, but you believe in yourself too. That bodes well for what is to come next," Louis said.

"And what exactly comes next?" I asked, looking from one man to the other.

"Jacob will be here shortly, and then the rest is really up to you," Roger said.

No sooner had he said that than my phone went off, alerting me that Jacob was on the premises.

"Well, here goes nothing," I said, getting up and going into the bathroom.

Without hesitation I pulled the gun from my clutch, laid my clutch on the sink, and chambered a round. I felt like years of target practice was about to get real, but I took the fact that my hands weren't shaking as a sign that I was okay with whatever came next. After what seemed like an eternity, I heard Jacob's voice signaling that their meeting had begun. Part of me wanted to rush out there guns blazing, but the objective was to get answers first, so I waited. I didn't know how long I'd planned to wait, but then I heard Jacob declare that he was in charge, the waiting was over, and all I could see was red. As quietly as I could I opened the bathroom door and crept into the room, gun outstretched in my right hand.

"Actually, I'm next in line," I declared, moving up on Jacob swiftly and putting the gun to his temple.

"Ivy what – what the fuck are you doing?"

"Isn't it obvious, Uncle Jacob? I'm joining the family business. My first act is getting rid of you," I replied calmly.

"Ivy, sweetheart, please talk to me and put that gun down."

"It's funny that you wanna talk, because that's what we had in mind too," Louis said.

"Wh-what is this about?" Jacob asked.

"Why didn't you stand up to the cartel with my father?" I asked.

"Ivy, I don't know what you've been told, but you don't understand this business, and - "

"But we understand the business, and we want the same question answered," Louis interjected.

"Soloman and I just had different views, but - "

"But nothing! You're supposed to stick together no matter what!" I growled angrily, pushing the barrel of the gun into his head harder.

"Ivy, listen, you don't understand - "

"Here's what I understand: my dad is gone because of you. Now take your phone out slowly and slide it to Mr. Jones. Don't make me ask twice," I warned.

He did as he was told without hesitation, but that wouldn't change the outcome.

"Louis, I want you to record this, but make sure you get his face only," I said, moving my gun to the back of his head.

"You want a taped confession?" Jacob asked.

"No, I want my dad back."

"We're recording," Louis said, pointing the phone at Jacob.

"To whoever has Soloman Black: return him or else," I said, pulling the trigger and spraying Jacob's beans across the table.

"Did you get that?" I asked.

"Uh-uh huh," Louis replied, visibly shaken.

"Good. Now give me the phone," I said, stepping around the table to retrieve it.

"Gentleman, per you request I'm now in charge, so let's discuss business. And since we're all family here, you can call me Ivy."

CHAPTER 10
SOLOMAN
THREE DAYS LATER...

I heard the footsteps approaching as I was finishing up my third set of 500 push-ups, and from the sound of it, there were more than two feet headed my way. It was too soon after my last feeding of slop to be meal time again, so this meant unexpected visitors. There was no masking the sweat or the fact that I'd been working out, but I chose to sit on my cot so as to appear non-threatening despite having more strength than they probably expected. The way the door opened and José came barreling through it, I knew something had happened to piss him the fuck off majorly. I wanted to smile, but not as badly as I wanted whatever info he came to deliver, so I kept the gloating to myself.

"Long time no see, José. I trust all is well."

"All is not fucking well, and if you don't fix it, I'm gonna blow your fucking head off," he replied angrily, putting his Taurus .357 in my face and cocking the hammer.

"I can only die once, and I'm not into a whole lot of freedom talking, so do what you gotta do," I said. Suddenly I had two more guns in my face courtesy of my captor, but I still didn't change my expression or cop any plea to spare my life. Frankly, this entire situation was getting old and I was sick of the bullshit.

"Do you think I won't kill you or let my men do it? We will kill you and - "

"And my family, and blah, blah, blah. Skip the bullshit and get to the reason you're really here," I said, fighting a yawn.

The look on José's face when he came in the room had been pissed, but now he had murder written all over his face.

His goons must've felt it too because they jumped on me before he could say a word. One was smacking me across the head with the butt of his pistol hard enough to scramble my vision instantly while the other used his gun to work on my rib cage. I tried balling up to ward of the blows, but it did me no good.

Just when I felt like I would lose consciousness, I heard him tell his men to stop, allowing me to finally cough up the blood I could taste in my mouth. For long moments I laid on the smelly cot wondering whether death or a coma would come first, but it seemed like José was too impatient for either because he was still looming over me.

"What – the – fuck – do – you – want?" I asked weakly.

"I want you to end this and do as you're told from now on. It's that simple," he said, pulling me back into a sitting position despite my muffled screams of pain.

A quick mental assessment of my injuries told me that at least two ribs were cracked or broken and my left eye was swelling shut fast, but my thought process hadn't slowed in the slightest.

"Do as I'm told? I don't work for you, and if you think that'll ever happen, then you better pull the trigger. I ain't no bitch like Jacob," I stated defiantly.

"So you're willing to destroy everything you've worked your whole life for? You've willing to leave your family with nothing and no way to protect themselves?" he asked.

"Despite what Jacob has done to me, he won't go near my family, so - "

"But he assured me he would, just a few days ago. So how did you get to him?"

"He said what? Wait, what do you mean how did I get to him?" I asked, confused.

"You know what the fuck I am talking about. He's dead, which has put a halt on our business. This does not help your position, so you need to tell your people to play ball."

I heard what he was saying, but I was still stuck on the fact that Jacob was dead. Had Big killed him, or maybe Rockafella? Nah, it didn't make sense for Rock to kill him because that would tear him and Ebony apart. So who did it?

"If Jacob is dead, I don't know anything about it. I mean, how could I, since you've had me locked away in this grimy-ass apartment?" I said reasonably.

"I don't know how the fuck you did it, but you need to get this shit straight so business can go back to running smoothly. It is the only way to stop Estéban from killing your family."

One thing I knew about Estéban was that he was a man of his word, and if he'd sent this message to me, then I had to consider my options.

"I can't make anything happen from here. You have to release me," I said.

"Do I look stupid to you? That is the same thing your puta demanded, but I promise you, there will be no consideration of your return until business resumes."

"That is what who demanded?" I asked, again confused.

In response he passed his gun to one of his men while pulling a phone from his jeans pocket. After a few steps on the screen he shoved the phone in my face so I could see the video playing. At first all I saw was Jacob sitting there with someone standing behind him, but at the same time that the camera zoomed in on his face, his head exploded. When José had said Jacob was dead I had my doubts, but this video was realer than Trump sitting in the white house, and just as unsettling. I'd done a lot of dirt, but I'd never had to bear witness to a man's thoughts as they oozed from what was left of his head. Especially not someone I once cared for.

"Why did you show me this? You can't even see the shooter," I said.

He pulled the phone back, tapped on the screen some more, and then shoved it back in my face. I started to object to seeing it again, but this time the audio was turned up. And I knew that voice.

"Again," I whispered, once the video had come to its end.

I didn't really wanna keep watching it, but there was no other way to believe what I was hearing. Immediately I prayed that she hadn't been the one to pull the trigger, even though I knew the prayer was in vain because I'd bought her the black Michael Kors cocktail dress that I now recognized standing behind Jacob. Somehow Ivy had put together what happened, and now she had blood on her hands.

"I can tell you recognize the voice, so I will allow you to make the necessary call. Because if you don't, I will find her myself and slit her throat from ear - "

In that moment I lost all control and before I knew it, my hands were around his throat, squeezing and dragging him to the floor with me. I could feel the weight of one of his henchmen collapse on me, but the sight of José's life draining from his eyes was the needed fuel to ignore the blows I was being hit with.

"Talk that shit now, bitch," I growled between clenched teeth, tightening my grip like a pitbull with lockjaw.

The way his mouth opened in a desperate attempt to get air was oddly fishlike, and even more insensitive to keep squeezing. No matter what happened I was determined that this mu'fucka would die at my hands for his betrayal and greed. Suddenly the punches and kicks stopped raining on me, allowing me to reposition for a more crushing grip, but my victory was short-lived.

A deafening noise erupted from behind me that immediately caused my hands to release José as my body was tossed off of his. It wasn't my first time being shot so I knew exactly what had happened, but the fact that I couldn't move any body part was new. All I could do was lay there in a growing pool of my own blood while I watched them fight to breathe life back into José. As the cold chill of death warned me, I prayed I'd see José on the other side so we could finish. Deep down I knew even if that didn't happen Ivy would avenge me, and that gave me a feeling of peace.

CHAPTER 11
EBONY

"Mom…I warmed you up some gumbo," I said, walking into the dimly-lit bedroom and setting the tray of food on her nightstand.

I knew she heard me, but she gave no outward signs of it because she just continued laying in the bed with her pistol in one hand and her bible in the other. I'd never known my mother to be an overly religious person, but ever since my father didn't show up when he said he would, she hadn't released her bible. Her gun either.

"Mom, you've gotta eat something," I pleaded.

For my efforts all I got was a slow blink as she continued staring at the ceiling. When I'd found her in this same position on the first day, I hadn't thought much of it, but by day two I had the doctor at the house checking her out. Of course, this pissed her off and she threatened to shoot the poor man, but it reassured me that she hadn't slipped into a catatonic state. All I could do was keep a close eye on her because I'd learned my lesson about calling anyone for help. The only good thing to come out of this was that having to look after her didn't leave time for me to fall apart. My father and I had our differences, but he was still my daddy and I'd be lost in this world without him.

"Mom, please eat something," I said, retreating the way I'd come so I could take my own advice. My mother and father had been together so long that I doubted she knew how to survive without him. I didn't know that I did either.

"How is she?" Rock asked as I came back into the kitchen.

"The same, laying there with her gun and bible."

"That means she's ready to do some biblical shit, like burn the world down," he replied seriously.

"I know. My dad might be away a lot, but when he says he'll be home he always is, and if not, he damn sure calls."

"I know, bae. I've got everyone global trying to locate him, but nobody knows where he went once he touched down from Mexico. There's no signal from the GPS in his phone or his truck either."

"What about whoever he was meeting in Mexico?" I asked, fixing myself a bowl of leftover gumbo and joining him at the kitchen table.

"I'm still trying to reach out to them."

"What was he working on down there anyway?" I asked.

"I don't know, bae. We do a lot of business in Mexico," he replied evasively.

I really had no interest in the business, so I wasn't about to press it. I just wanted to retrace my dad's steps.

"Maybe we should just go to Mexico," I suggested.

"Nah, that ain't a good move right now."

"Why not?" I asked.

"Because from what I've been able to gather, your dad's disappearance has put a stop to some big business, and mu'fuckas ain't happy about that. Trust me, there are a lot of people looking for Jacob, which means you don't gotta be on the front line."

"It's my father though!" I replied, frustrated at not being able to do anything to help.

"I know, bae, and I'm doing everything I can. Right now, you've gotta help your mom because no one else can do that."

I knew he was right about that, but I still didn't like this helpless feeling. I had to stay busy to not allow the fear in because once that happened, I'd be a victim to it and it could paralyze me like it had my mom. For a few minutes we ate in silence while I worked up the courage to put the bad taste in my mouth with my next question.

"So, what have you heard about Ivy?" I asked.

"They're still in Fort Worth."

"What did Big say when you talked to him?"

"I, uh, didn't talk to Big," he said hesitantly.

"What do you mean? Why wouldn't you talk to him, so he could have his people out looking for my father too?"

"For one, all his people are still looking for Soloman and I just had to pull my people off of that. For two, if you actually believe what you told me the other night, then I need to check some shit out before I contact him," he replied.

I could understand the logic in that because what I'd told him was that I didn't believe Ivy's phone call or the statement she made about my father's safety were coincidental to his disappearance. That bitch knew something.

"Is Ivy back to ignoring your messages?" he asked.

"Yeah, she's ducking me, but I'ma pop up on that bitch."

"Bae, I already told you, no matter what you two are going through at the moment, the love is still there. Plus, you're just alike, which means you wouldn't have shit to do with her father's disappearance any more than she would yours," he reasoned.

What he said made sense because neither of us was 'bout that life, but I still couldn't shake my distrust of her right now.

"Whatever. I need a distraction, so come on," I said, grabbing his hand and pulling him up from the table.

I could feel the resistance in his grip, but that was because he hated to leave that good-ass bowl of gumbo. I had something better than that for him, and I know he quickly figured that out when we arrived at our destination of the first floor half-bathroom.

"Hold up, bae - "

"Shhh, no talking," I commanded, pulling him inside, locking the door, and pushing him up against the sink.

When he opened his mouth, I knew it was to speak, but his thoughts froze when I reached inside his sweatpants and grabbed his dick. He wasn't hard, but I knew how to fix that. Dropping to my knees, I took him into my mouth and began humming while my right hand played with his balls gently. With each passing second, I could feel him growing and coming to life in my mouth, which encouraged me to suck from the base of his shaft to the tip of his head and slowly back down. Quicker than gunfire on New Year's Eve, his dick was hard and throbbing in my mouth, which meant the real work could begin.

"Now fuck me," I demanded, switching places with him, dropping my shorts to my ankles and bending over the sink.

I could see the look of hesitation on his face from his reflection in the mirror, but like any man, he went from looking me in the eye to looking at the pussy and ass staring at him. Ordinarily I'd tell him the ass was off limits, but right now I just needed to feel anything except the hole that was growing inside me.

"Put your dick in me," I said, backing up on him further until he had no choice except to grab my hips.

From that point I didn't have a chance to take a deep breath before he made my kitty purr in delight. I didn't just let him fuck me though. I matched him stroke for stroke, throwing it and taking it, loving that I had his dick throbbing in surrender within minutes. The harder he pounded me, the faster I threw that ass back to get more, feeding off the echoed sounds of our skin slapping in this tiny space. I was just about to crest the first wave of a tsunami-sized orgasm when he suddenly stopped.

"Wh-what the fuck, bae, why you stop?" I panted, still trying to grind on him in hot pursuit of that ghost that would rattle my knees.

"Are you okay?" he asked slowly.

The worry and fear in his voice caused me to look at him in the mirror, and it wasn't until then that I saw the wetness on my cheeks. I was crying, and I hadn't noticed, but he had, and the look on his face was complete terror.

"I-I'm fine, just keep going," I said, but I could already feel him pulling out of me and turning me around to face him.

"Bae, what is it? Did I hurt you? Because if I did, I'm sorry. I didn't mean to."

"I'm f-fine," I insisted, trying to fight the sob in my throat.

When he pulled me into his arms, I finally lost the fight and I cried in a way I hadn't since I was a child. I tried taking a deep breath so I could explain the tears, but I was ugly crying now and way beyond talking. Thankfully I had a man who truly loved me and so he just held me and allowed me to get snot and tears all over his shirt. After a solid five minutes of blubbering like an idiot, I was finally able to gather enough self-control to be completely embarrassed by what just happened.

"I'm so-so sorry, I just - "

"Shhh. You don't owe me any explanation, bae, especially not with all you're going through," he reassured me, gently stroking my hair and holding me tighter.

"I just didn't want you to think you were hur-hurting me."

"Baby, I know I've got good dick, but it ain't never hurt you before," he said, chuckling.

His comment made me laugh too, and I loved him more in this moment than I ever had. Once I'd gathered my composure, I stepped back a little so I could reach up and pull his lips to mine.

"I know I look a hot-ass mess right now, but - "

"You're beautiful," he said, kissing first the tears on my left cheek and then my right before bringing his mouth back to mine.

I could taste the salt, but even more than that I could taste the love he had for me, and that reignited the fires below. This time when I took his dick in my hand I was gentle with it, letting my fingers walk over it like it contained a message of love covered in Braille. When his hands went to my ass cheeks, I quickly kicked one leg free of my shorts so when he lifted me up on the sink I could spread my legs wide in welcome. His journey through the gates of my heaven was slow and steady this go around, almost painful in the way he pushed only an inch in at a time until we were joined as one.

"Baby, fuck - "

"Shhh, I got this," he whispered into my mouth, setting a pace that allowed for the rough exploration of my treasure chest.

Locking my legs behind his back brought us closer still, my moans now riding the air with each punctuated stroke. I wanted him to go faster, but the thrills he was giving me made actual words impossible. Suddenly his hand was around my throat, tilting me back up against the mirror, forcing my legs to go from around his back to around his neck. Now his pace did increase, causing it to feel like his dick was in my stomach and bringing my orgasm from its hiding spot with blinding speed.

"Oh fuck!" I cried out, drenching him in my juices as wave after wave pushed me under.

I could feel another one coming as he slammed into me harder, when the sound of a gunshot shattered our concentration.

"What the fuck was that?" I asked, pushing against him so he'd let me off the counter.

Before he could answer I heard my mother screaming and I didn't waste any time bolting out of the bathroom asshole naked.

"Wait!" Rock yelled, but I was already taking the stairs two at a time. I didn't give a fuck what awaited me in my mom's room. I just knew I had to get there in a hurry.

"Mom!" I yelled, rushing through the door to find her sitting up stone still in her bed with her gun in one hand and her phone in the other.

Looking around, I didn't spot anyone else in the room, but the bullet hole in the ceiling explained the gunshot I heard.

"Mom! Mom, what's wrong?" I asked, rushing to her side.

Had the situation not been so serious, I would've been mortified to stand this close to her smelling freshly fucked, but I needed to know what was going on.

"Mom, talk to me. Please."

The glassy far off look in her eyes had me more worried than anything had over the past few days because it looked like the life had literally left her body. Whatever had happened, I could tell she couldn't tell me, but I had a hunch that her phone would. I reached to take it from her grasp and that's when I found myself looking down the barrel of her pistol.

"M-Mom. Mommy, what are you doing? It's me," I said, slowly backing away and putting my hands in the air.

She was looking at me, but I could tell she wasn't seeing me.

"Mom, it's me. It's - "

"Whoa, what the fuck, Mrs. Dahl?" Rock said, coming through the door.

She quickly swung the gun in his direction, but luckily, she fired before actually aiming, which made the bullet go wide.

"Mom!" I screamed as Rock hit the floor and rolled back out of the door. The shrill sound of my voice snapped her out of whatever padded room her mind had locked itself in because when she looked back at me, I actually saw my mom. "Tell me what happened," I demanded.

This time she pushed the phone at me before dropping her gun and dissolving into a puddle of tears. She wasn't just crying though. She was wailing from her soul, and that fear that I'd just shaken off downstairs came back in full force. Now I didn't wanna look at the cell phone, but I knew I had to. Just looking at the screen I could see my dad's face, and the suit he had on was the last one I saw him in, which meant the video was recent.

After several deep breaths I worked up the courage to press play, but within seconds, I'd wished I hadn't. Seeing my father's head explode caused me to vomit all over the phone and bed right before I felt myself falling from an impossible height. By the time my head bounced off the carpeted floor, my mother's wailing was only a faint sound in the distance, and I welcomed the darkness rushing towards me.

I don't know how long I was out, but the feeling of cold water covering me from head to toe snatched me back from whatever peace I had.

"What the fuck!" I yelled, swatting uselessly at the cold shower raining down on me.

"You passed out. I understand why though," Rock said softly.

Immediately the memory came flooding back, making me wanna throw up again. But knowing the truth kept it down.

"Th-the video. The voice. The gun. It was - "

"I know, bae. It was Ivy."

CHAPTER 12
IVY

"You look better," Big said, as I came into the kitchen and went to the refrigerator.

"I feel a little better after that nap and a shower."

"Nap? Babe, you slept damn near thirty-six hours."

"Yeah, well…"

I let the rest of my thought go and just grabbed the ginger ale I was looking for before heading back to my dad's office. I was appreciative of the sleep because after what I'd done, I'd had my doubts about ever closing my eyes again without seeing Jacob. I'd managed to hold it together in front of my dad's associates, but once I got back in Big's truck, I came all the way unglued. I couldn't even explain what happened. I simply pushed the phone at him and let him see it for himself.

The whole ride home I kept trying to convince myself that I'd done what was necessary to get my dad back, but that hadn't stopped the shaking in my hands. That first night, I couldn't stand to face my own mother, even though she was unconscious, and the shaking had turned into my whole body trembling, so we just locked ourselves in the house. Big said it was shock and it would wear off, but until I'd actually got some sleep, I hadn't really believed him. It had felt like I was losing my fucking mind.

Now, in the night of day after much needed rest, I didn't know how I felt honestly. Jacob was someone I'd loved and trusted my whole life, someone I considered family, and I'd killed him. There was no coming back from that.

"We gotta talk," Big said, entering the office moments behind me.

"Talk," I replied, sitting in my father's chair behind his massive oak desk, sipping my soda.

"I sent the video to the cartel, but I still ain't get a response. I had to do it from a new burner phone since I destroyed Jacob's along with the truck."

"It doesn't matter what number it comes from because the message is clear. I want my dad back," I stated simply.

"I know, babe, and I've got every man under my command working on that. I'ma be real with you though. We're going up against some heavy hitters."

"I know. Just like I know that I'm as ruthless and cold-hearted as he was," I said.

"Oh, that video definitely gets that point across. It's about more than that though because now it's business and personal. Right now, nobody is making money, and that's bad for both sides so we gotta do some damage control."

"Such as?" I asked, putting my soda aside and giving him my full attention.

"For starters, because Jacob was so focused on the new business, he didn't bother to secure the re-up dope. If we ain't supplying dope to our customers they're gonna go elsewhere to get it, which means we lose both money and territory."

"Okay…money talks, right? So why can't we go to somebody else to get our dope?" I asked.

"Because the Sinaloa Cartel will take that as disrespect and - "

"I don't give a fuck how they take it. Them mu'fuckas got my dad! They took him, and I'm supposed to let them take his business too?" I asked heatedly.

"Nah, babe, that's not what I'm saying. I'm simply telling you what an act of war is so there's no misunderstanding any move you make."

I knew he was telling the truth and trying to be helpful, so I took a deep breath and counted to ten in my head before I said anything else.

"I know you're helping me, and thank you. But if you really wanna help me, then you have to teach me how to be completely heartless like the niggas who own these streets and the Mexicans who supply them. I know you love me and wanna protect me, but the only way to do that is to give me the game," I explained patiently. I could see so many different emotions swim through his chocolate brown eyes, but he quickly tucked all that away as he reached the conclusion that what I was asking had to be done.

"I got you, babe, but it's some shit that has to be shown and not talked about, so get dressed."

"Why? Where we going?" I asked.

"We gotta show everyone who the new boss is, and that starts with dealing with the traitors in this organization."

The look in his eyes now was that of a shark, which told me more than his statement had. Traitors were dealt with harshly, and with me being in charge now, that meant I had to be the one to deal with these kinds of problems. Eventually it would get to the point where I could delegate certain responsibilities, but that only came after I had some respect on my name. Gaining my respect in the business arena wasn't hard, but to do it in the street meant blood had to be spilled.

"I'm assuming I need to dress down for this," I said, standing up.

"Whatever is gonna make you comfortable."

I headed upstairs to find something to wear out of the clothes I kept here for emergencies. I could've went with sweats since I had a few pair that I lounged in, but that wasn't me. Ten minutes later I came back downstairs in a navy blue Zac Posen pants suit with six inch stilettos covered in jewels.

"Are you really wearing no shirt or bra under that blazer?" Big asked, licking his lips unconsciously.

"That's never bothered you before. Don't let it now," I replied, picking up the silver and black 9mm Glock he had laid out on the table and tucking it into the back of my pants.

"Can you tell I'm carrying?" I asked, doing a slow twirl for him.

"I can tell you've got beautiful titties and I don't want everybody staring at them."

"Then I guess we'll have to make sure that business is everyone's number one priority. Right?"

The look on his face said this nigga wanted to drag me back upstairs and physically change my outfit if necessary, but he knew that effortless sexy was my everyday look, and he'd told me to be authentic.

"Right," he agreed through clenched teeth, grabbing the matching Glock and leading the way outside.

It was no surprise to me that there was a mob of niggas waiting out front because ever since I'd killed Jacob, Big had stepped up security in a major way. It wasn't something I liked, but I understood the need for it. We didn't know who to trust right now so Big surrounded us with people he'd bet his life on.

"Okay, so run this situation down to me," I said once we were in the back seat of my father's black 2017 H2 hummer.

The change of vehicles had been my decision because I knew this one was armored.

"Remember when I told you that we'd come down here for a meeting because some shit had been happening? Well, we were taking losses, big losses of both product and money. Even though your pops got taken, my people still kept digging because we figured it had to be somebody on the inside."

"So someone from our organization was stealing from us?" I asked.

"Yes and no. It's actually a collaboration between one of my people, one of Rock's people, and a Sinaloa Cartel member."

"I'm assuming wherever we're going all three of these mu'fuckas are. My only question is, what does Rock have to say about his man and what happens next?" I asked.

"I didn't ask him. And don't give me that look because you know that confiding in him ain't the right move for us right now. Babe, I love you, and if I had to choose between you and anybody else, who do you think I'd choose?"

With that question, I understood exactly what he was saying. Rockafella was literally sleeping with the enemy now, and eventually they would come to feel the same way about us. What was once a happy family was now a house divided. The truth in that hurt my heart because I could've never imagined anything in the world that would separate Ebony and me. Life wasn't always lived based on the plans we made though.

"Alright, so where are we going, and what happens when we get there?" I asked, focusing on the business at hand.

"We're going to a spot we got in Waco, out in the middle of nowhere. What happens when we get there is up to you."

"Oh, so you can advise me about my wardrobe, but not this?" I asked sarcastically.

"You don't need my advice. You know what has to be done. I'll warn you now though that because the mu'fuckas who worked for me and Rock had what equates to the rank of lieutenant in our organizations, they have to be dealt with in public."

"What do you mean in public?" I asked, knowing the odds of getting away with a daytime shooting were slim to none. Everything was recorded these days.

"I mean in front of everybody under their command. This way it's known from top to bottom how you handle business."

What he was suggesting wasn't any more appealing, but I understood it was necessary. The remainder of the hour-long ride was spent with me trying to figure out how to best approach this situation, since my arsenal of war tactics was admittedly weak. When we pulled up to the ranch style house surrounded by neglected and overgrown farmland, I still didn't have a clear idea of what to do. My only option was to play it by ear.

"Where is everyone?" I asked, noticing no cars parked on the premises.

"Inside. I ordered everyone to be dropped off so they couldn't leave until you said so. If you said so."

"Smart thinking. I don't wanna be crowded in that house though, so bring everyone outside," I instructed.

When he got out of the car to make that happen, I pulled the pistol from the small of my back and checked to make sure it was ready for action. Within a couple minutes niggas started stumbling out of the front door into the yard, fifteen in all, including the three mu'fuckas bound and gagged that were led like cattle. It wasn't hard to tell that most of the spectators weren't feeling the idea of their homies being led to slaughter, but the Mexican got no love. That made my first move an easy one. Taking a deep breath, I opened the door and stepped out into the bright afternoon sun.

"I want them three on their knees," I instructed, sauntering towards the crowd in a way that demanded all eyes be focused on me.

I knew the first impression was the most important one, and so there was no need to act like I didn't know how good I looked. I wouldn't let that stand in the way of my respect though. Without a word I stopped in front of the Mexican, put my gun to the middle of his forehead, and pulled the trigger. I heard a few people say "Oh shit" as the crowd took a collective step back, and all eyes focused on me in a different way.

"Before we finish what we came here for, allow me to introduce myself. My name is Ivy Black, and Soloman is my father. While he's away I'll be in control of everything, and I expect shit to run as smoothly as it did when he was at the helm. If you feel like my beauty or the fact that I have a pussy somehow makes me unfit to lead this movement, I urge you to reconsider," I said, taking aim at the man kneeling to my left and pulling the trigger, scattering his thoughts to the wind.

"Now, the two gentlemen dead before you thought it was a good idea to steal from my father, but I guarantee they aren't thinking that anymore. Before I shoot this last disloyal piece of shit, I would like to explain the obvious for those still unclear on why this is happening. You're paid, and you're paid well because everybody eats, but there's a reason that greed is a sin. I know these gentlemen might've been your friend or your brother, but they betrayed you the same way they did me. Their actions could've cost you your lives or your families' lives, and you didn't even get a cut. So, you can be bitter about this or you can understand it for what it is. Just remember that one monkey doesn't stop no show," I concluded, turning my gun on the final man kneeling and pulling the trigger twice.

Once his body dropped I turned around to go back to the truck, but I stopped short and turned back to the still-stunned crowd.

"Any questions?" I asked. I gave it a full ten count in my head before continuing on my way and climbing into the backseat.

"Damn, you cold! Big never told me you were that cold," his cousin said, looking at me in the rearview mirror from the driver's seat.

"I do what I gotta do," I replied, setting the gun on the seat next to me and folding my hands in my lap to hide the shaking.

Part of my brain wanted to deny what I'd just done, but all I had to do was look straight through the windshield at the bodies leaking blood and brain matter into the soil. Who was I becoming, and was it someone I could live with? Deep down I knew the answers to those questions wouldn't come until much later. All I could do was hope it wasn't too late by then. I know Big would take control of the meeting and deliver instructions because that was his job. He was what stood between me and the streets. But all of a sudden, he stopped talking to take a call, and when he looked straight through the windshield at me, my heart leapt into my throat. I didn't know what it was, but whatever it was, it wasn't good. He quickly dismissed the group and headed straight for the truck.

"What is it?" I asked, before he'd even climbed in.

"Let's go," he said to his cousin, ignoring me.

"Big, what is it?" I asked, praying it wasn't my father.

"Where are we going?" his cousin asked.

"The hospital," he replied, taking my hand.

CHAPTER 13
EBONY

"Bae, we need to talk."

"What you wanna talk about?" I asked, covering my eyes because of the light he'd just let into my room by opening the curtains.

"Ever since your dad - "

"We're not talking about that," I said forcefully.

"Bae, you can't just avoid it."

"Sure I can," I replied, fumbling around on my nightstand until I found my sunglasses and put them on.

"I know you're hurting, sweetheart, but your dad wouldn't want - "

"I said we're not talking about this!" I repeated, raising my voice and sitting up in my bed.

I loved Rock, but at the moment I couldn't stand the sight of him, so I focused on the bottle on my nightstand calling my name. Vodka for breakfast was better than sex, I'd discovered, and it was less work too.

"You're trippin'. Drinking all day ain't gonna change the shit that's going on around you," he said.

"No, but it'll change how I see it," I replied, tipping the bottle to my lips and taking a swig.

Rock didn't understand. I just wanted to ever hurt again.

"So, you're just gonna be a fucking alcoholic? Real sexy, Ebony."

"Thank you," I said, burping loudly, much to his annoyance.

"The way to honor your father ain't to throw your life away, especially doing the one thing he hated you doing."

"If you're gonna lecture me, just get out," I said, taking another healthy drink from the half-empty bottle.

"Or maybe you should get out," my mom said, coming into the bedroom.

"Wh-what?" I asked, confused.

"You heard me, Ebony. You can either put down the bottle or get the fuck out of my house, and I mean that."

"Oooh, Marissa is angry with me," I replied, laughing at the stern expression on her face as I took another drink.

I didn't really know how much time had passed since my best friend had taken my life from me, but I couldn't remember the last time I'd seen my mom upright. It might've been the liquor, but she looked halfway normal.

"Rockafella, get her out of here." my mom ordered.

"I'm not leaving. This is my daddy's house, and I - "

I didn't get the rest of the sentence out before she'd advanced on me and slapped me hard enough to send the bottle and its contents flying across the room. Through the sunglasses sitting crookedly on my face I suddenly saw my mother in a different light because she never put her hands on me.

"Newsflash, you spoiled little bitch. This is my house. Jacob was my husband, and that means you don't lay claim to shit unless I allow it. Understand?"

"M-mom, I - "

"Understand?" she asked again, moving as if to take another swing at me.

"I understand."

"Good," she replied in a gentler tone, sitting next to me on the bed. "Nobody understands your pain the way that I do, sweetheart, but we can't let that destroy us. Not now. Your father always knew and acknowledged the risks to the game, so he knew he was constantly playing with borrowed time. That in no way justifies that bitch killing him, but it should help us understand that we knew this could happen one day. We've gotta keep pushing though, baby, for your dad's sake."

By now I was a puddle of tears with my head in her lap, reminiscent of my younger years when she used to console me. In those days no matter how bad shit got, I knew it would get better, but I didn't know that to be true anymore. My daddy was everything to both of us, the life source of this family. How would we survive without that? For what seemed like hours I laid in my mother's lap, asking myself the same question until I finally ran out of tears to shed.

"We'll be okay, baby," my mom assured me.

"But how?" I asked, looking up to find tears rolling down her face like giant raindrops.

"Because we have each other. Because we've never been weak women. And because your father would want it no other way."

I knew every word she spoke was the truth, just as surely that I knew it wouldn't be easy to live with the huge hole in my heart. There would never be a second when I wasn't missing my daddy, but I couldn't waste seconds dishonoring his memory either. I had more important shit to do. Slowly I sat up, hoping I didn't upset the liquor in my stomach because I really didn't feel like throwing up again. I also needed a few seconds to organize my thoughts before I spoke them aloud.

"Mom?"

"Yes, sweetheart?"

"I wanna kill her," I stated calmly.

"I do too, but - "

"No, no buts. What I mean to say is that I'm going to kill her," I said, determination radiating from my soul.

For a few seconds she simply looked at me, and then she turned to Rock. Without another word she got up from the bed and walked out of the room.

"What was that?" I asked, looking quizzically at Rock.

"She wanted to tell you not to kill her, but she can't. So she's hoping I will, but either way she doesn't wanna know."

"You got all that from one look?" I asked skeptically.

"I know this from conversations we've had while you were drinking yourself in and out of consciousness. Your mom may have accepted your dad's lifestyle, but that's not how she lives her life. When she finally got ahold of herself, her first instinct was to call the police and then hand the video over to them."

"But if she did that, they'd have to look into my dad's life," I concluded.

"Exactly, and that's what I told her. I also told her that this has to be handled in the street."

"So, you're not gonna tell me not to kill her?" I asked, somewhat surprised.

"No, I'm actually gonna help you."

"Help me? What about Big Cuzz? You know he - "

"I don't give a fuck how he feels. It's Global Gangsta or nothing with me from now on," he said passionately.

Right away I knew I'd missed something, but there was no way I could absorb information in my current state.

"Bae, I need you to make me some coffee while I take a shower. Please?" I asked, knowing that I was gonna have to pay for my bad behavior.

"I got you," he replied, leaving me alone to box with my demons.

After a few deep breaths for preparation, I slowly got off the bed and made my way into my bathroom, stripping my clothes off as I went. Turning on the shower, I hopped in while it was still cold in order to shock my senses and then I let the blistering heat push some of the alcohol out of my pores. I could actually smell myself and that made me want to vomit more than all the alcohol consumption.

Apparently, I hadn't taken a shower since my bathroom escapade with Rock, and the funk of sex wasn't sexy days later. After an hour of scrubbing myself until my skin was damn near raw, I finally felt decent enough to get out and begin the process of figuring out my life. Taking it one day at a time wasn't possible yet, so I'd have to move from moment to moment and hope I didn't fall apart. When I stepped from the bathroom naked, Rock was standing there with my towel in one hand and my coffee in the other.

"Thanks," I said, taking the towel first, avoiding eye contact because I was sober enough to be ashamed of my behavior. "Rock, I - "

"I know, bae. We're good, I promise," he said, kissing me on the forehead and passing me the still hot coffee.

I used the cup to hide my smile, taking a small sip to see how my stomach would react. With no immediate rumblings I continued drinking, going to my closet to find something to wear. There was no way in hell I was going full on dress up, so I grabbed a cream-colored Gucci blouse and some black Gucci slacks before I could change my mind.

"How long have I been in my own world?" I asked, tossing the clothes on my bed and sitting at my vanity to deal with my bird's nest of curly hair.

"A week."

"A week!" I exclaimed, looking at him in the mirror to see if he was fucking with me.

"Yes, a week. I can't lie and say you didn't scare the shit out of me, but the way you were acting is actually what brought your mom out of her funk."

"A week though," I said again in disbelief.

"You were throwed, bae, and given what you saw, I had to be somewhat understanding."

My disbelief quickly disappeared as I looked at myself closer in the mirror because it looked like that week had added five years to my life. I was too young to have these kinds of bags under my eyes and stress lines on my face!

"Oh wow," I murmured, setting the coffee cup down and reaching for the things needed to right this wrong.

To my delighted surprise, Rock grabbed one of my brushes and gently went to work untangling the mess on top of my head.

"If you ever try to tell this story to our kids one day, I'll deny it," he said in response to the look I was giving him in the mirror.

The smile I gave him was genuine and it felt good to do that, but it didn't last long.

"Tell me what I missed," I said.

"Well, not only did Ivy do what she did, but she also executed three people who were discovered to be stealing from us. One of them was a homie under my command."

His statement brought into perspective why he was more than willing to help me kill Ivy, but I hurt for him because I knew he was dealing with multiple losses like I was.

"I'm assuming you weren't consulted before this went down. So what does this mean, Ivy's taking over the business now?" I asked.

"From what I've been told that's exactly what it means, and Big is backing her play."

What he said didn't really make sense to me because I know Ivy had no interest in the business whatsoever. Then again, I'd known she'd never do anything to hurt me or my family, and now I'd seen first-hand how wrong I was about that assumption.

"It sounds like you're saying Ivy killed my father to take the business over."

My statement didn't solicit the immediate response I was expecting. It actually made him look away from me in the mirror, which told me there was more I didn't know.

"You need to tell me everything, Rock," I said, pausing in my make-up routine.

"Ivy didn't go after Jacob for the business. That was purely about revenge. My guess is that someone put the pieces of what happened to Soloman together for Ivy, and inheriting the business was just collateral damage."

"Wait, what do you mean put the pieces together about Soloman?" I asked, confused.

"Soloman's disappearance wasn't just random selection between him and your dad. Your dad was in on it. I only knew that because he told me of his plans to be the only king over this kingdom. I never repeated that conversation until now, but it wouldn't be hard to surmise that Jacob had at the very least sided with the cartel's agenda over what Soloman wanted. From there it's not that big of a leap to his betrayal, but I don't think he anticipated Ivy making that leap or acting on it if she did. Neither did I," he admitted.

I had no immediate words for what I'd just heard. I was literally speechless at the knowledge that this entire nightmare started with my own father's actions. How was that possible? My father had raised me to understand the importance of absolute, unwavering loyalty above all else, so how could I now question this? If this story had come from anyone other than Rock I wouldn't believe a word of it, but I could see the truth all over his face. It was obvious to both of us that I had a decision to make.

"Did you tell my mother what you just told me?" I asked.

"Of course not. She's not gonna understand a street war or the politics that governs it."

"Is there a war still going on?" I asked.

"There is, and the Sinaloa Cartel had the upper hand until Ivy got into business with the Gulf Cartel. Plus, she has the support of all Hoovers across Texas."

"But not your people, right?" I asked, a plan starting to slowly take shape in my mind.

"I'm not supporting them, and Big knows better than to ask."

"Well, Ivy can't just take over a business that both of our fathers built, and right or wrong, she can't get away with killing my dad," I vowed.

"So, what do you wanna do?"

"I want that bitch," I replied simply.

"Are you willing to do whatever it takes to get her?"

"Is that even a real question?" I asked, looking him in the eyes.

"It is because I know how to get her, but we have to move on it today."

I could tell he was deadly serious, but my heart knew not a moment's hesitation. "I want her," I stated emphatically.

In response he tossed my brush aside, put my hair in a quick ponytail, and pulled out his phone. After searching for something for a few minutes, he turned the screen towards me to look at. I could taste the bile in my throat instantly at what he was suggesting, but my eyes didn't leave the screen. Two words came to my mind: poetic justice.

"Is this really the only way?" I asked.

"This business ain't for the soft-hearted, bae. It's clear that Ivy has already figured that out, so what are you gonna do?"

Part of me couldn't believe I was even contemplating this insanity, but the other part knew that if I closed my eyes I'd still see my father's head missing. That was the part I had to tap into.

"Do you have a plan?" I asked.

"Follow me to the garage really quick."

I traded my towel for my silk bathrobe, tying the belt tight at the waist and following him outside to the barn that had been converted into a multi-car garage. When I walked through the huge sliding door, I was surprised to find a mini-van I'd never seen.

"Are you a soccer mom now?" I asked sarcastically.

"Funny, smart ass, but peep inside."

When I did, what I saw left my jaw extended to its full potential because my mouth was hanging wide open.

"How's that gonna work?" I asked, fascinated.

Suddenly the sliding doors on both sides of the van, and the back door, all opened at the same time. Without waiting for an invitation, I climbed into the back and sat in the chair that had been specially mounted to the vans floor in place of the bench seats that came stock. After strapping into the safety harness, the chair gained the ability to swivel and given the added accessories, I now understood how it was possible to pull off Rock's plan.

"This shit is gonna get real," I predicted, turning the chair to face him.

"It's been real. Now it's time to show them that."

CHAPTER 14
IVY

"The lord giveth and taketh away. No one knows the time or place when we will be called home to his side, but it is not a time for sadness because death is a part of life. It is life's reward. I know we all wish Margarita didn't receive her reward so soon, but we must seek solace in the fact that her worldly suffering ended with the beginning of her everlasting life. She will be deeply missed, yet never forgotten. At this time, I'm gonna ask her lovely daughter Ivy to say a few words," the preacher concluded, looking in my direction.

I knew that I needed to step forward and say something before I tossed the first fistful of dirt onto her coffin, but I couldn't move because I didn't know what to say. Even with Big holding my hand and the closest of friends and family gathered around the gravesite, I still felt utterly and completely alone. I wasn't ready to say goodbye to my mother. I didn't know how! I needed her, I needed her now more than I ever had in my entire life, so how was I supposed to say goodbye?

"You can do this," Big whispered in my ear, giving me a quick kiss on the cheek and squeezing my hand before letting it go.

I prayed he was right as I forced my feet to move forward. I was thankful for my sunglasses because I didn't really want anyone to see how distraught I was. Or how guilty I felt.

"There are no words to describe what my mother means to me, so there's no words I can use to say goodbye. When she got the terminal diagnosis from the doctor, she made me promise not to be sad on this day, but we both knew I'd be lying because losing her is losing part of myself. If you would've told me a month ago that my life would be what it is now, there's no way I would've believed you, but God makes the plans and the rules. I hope he's also made room for my parents because they deserve to be up there happy together. My mom was such a good person, and she loved everybody. Mommy, I love you. And Daddy…"

At this point, the tears in my throat could no longer be held in, and the ugly crying commenced. I was grateful that Big pulled me into the arms and just let me pour my heart out in the form of gut-wrenching sobs. The truth was that the cartel hadn't confirmed that my dad was dead, but they hadn't returned him, and the proof of life pictures stopped going to Jacob's email account. The only communication exchanged between us in the last week had been bullets. The biggest sign for me had been my mom slipping from her coma into whatever waited beyond the world because I firmly believed she only gave up after she knew my dad was gone. So today was the day to say I loved them both, but it was too hard.

"I c-can't," I wailed into Big's chest, holding him tightly to keep myself from falling.

"It's okay, bae. Come on," he said, turning me towards the truck so we could leave.

Before we could take a step, though, I caught sight of something I couldn't believe through my watery vision. Twenty feet away from the gravesite sat three black Caravans, all with their sliding doors open and some type of chair bolted in the place of the normal seats. If that wasn't weird enough, the arms of the chairs were 30mm belt-fed machine guns. As I looked closer, though, weird became disbelief because sitting in one chair was none other than Ebony herself. I opened my mouth to scream just as the barrels started glowing and all hell broke loose. Suddenly I was being shoved, and before I knew it I was landing with a solid smack on top of my mother's coffin. The ground may have been shielding me from the bullets, but it did nothing to drown out the noise of gunfire, screams, and death happening right about me.

"Big!" I screamed, seeing him return fire as he backed out of my view.

At first, I'd objected to him bringing his homies to my mom's service, but the sound of defensive fire was music to my ears, even if it was no match for the automatic rounds that were roaring like a very loud machine. My own gun was in the truck, but I still wasn't about to lay in this hole helpless. Just as I sank my hand into the fresh earth to pull myself out, the preacher's body came flying over my head into the hole with me. Before I could make a move to help him, I realized that it was futile because he had literally lost his head, and that caused me to lose my breakfast at his feet.

"Big!" I screamed again, wiping my mouth.

I doubted he could hear me over the endless gunfire, but the fear of losing him too was clawing at my throat. Finally, I heard the sounds of engines revving and the shots began to fade and move from over me at the same time. After what seemed like hours, Big's cousin appeared over the grave and reached down to pull me out.

"Don't look around. Just get to the truck," he said, hustling me in the direction.

I tried doing exactly what he said, but there were literally bodies everywhere that we had to navigate like a maze.

"Wh-where's Big?" I asked, trying not to stumble.

"In the truck."

My first thought was how was this nigga gonna run to the damn truck after he knew he'd pushed me into my mother's grave? But as soon as I opened the back door and saw him, my question was answered.

"Oh God, oh God, no!" I cried, scrambling up next to him in the seat.

"It's okay, it's j-just my arm," he panted.

"Hospital, hospital now!" I screamed at his cousin.

Within seconds we were moving at a high rate of speed, making it hard to locate the wound and stop the bleeding, but I was determined because I wouldn't lose him.

"Ahhhh!" he screamed, letting me know I'd located the bullet hole in my blind search.

"I know it hurts, but I gotta keep pressure on it," I said, quickly peeling off the blazer I was wearing over my black dress and jamming it up against his arm.

The sight of so much blood was threatening to send me into a blind panic, and the smell of it was making my stomach lurch harder than the wild-ass rate we were experiencing at the hands of Big's cousin. Still, I kept pressure on his wound and prayed we'd get to the hospital before he bled out.

"I-I saw them," Big said, grimacing in pain.

"Them? I only saw Ebony's bitch ass."

"Rock was there too, strapped into one of those chairs," he said, trying to reach in his pocket for something.

"Stay still goddammit!" I yelled at him.

"M-my phone, babe, get my phone."

"Fuck your phone right now! All I'm worried about is you," I said, fighting to hold back the endless wave of tears that were threatening to rob me of my voice.

Finally, we pulled up to the hospital and within seconds, the door on Big's side was opened by two nurses.

"He's been shot in the arm. I-I've been keeping pressure on the wound, but he's lost a lot of blood," I informed them.

"Okay, we got it from here," one female said while helping him ease out of the truck and onto the waiting stretcher.

I followed him straight out of the truck and was holding his hand before his head could rest on the stretcher.

"Ma'am, you have to stay out of the way so we can help him," the other nurse said.

In that moment, it took everything in me not to snatch both of these females bald, but I knew that would be counterproductive.

"If anything happens to him, I'm burying the both of you bitches," I promised.

"B-babe, my phone," Big said again.

This time I did reach into his pocket and grab it as they started wheeling him inside.

"Hoover Slim!" he yelled at me before disappearing behind the emergency room doors.

"Who is Hoover Slim?" I asked, turning to his cousin.

"He's a big homie and a friend. He'll wanna know what happened."

"You make that call, Marcus. I'm going in here with Big," I said, passing him the phone.

"I-I didn't know you knew my name," he said, more stunned by that than what had taken place today.

"Really, my nigga? Now ain't the time for formal introductions, so can you handle the business or not?"

"Yea, I can handle it, but you don't need to go in there right now," he replied cautiously.

"Before I cuss you out for having the nerve to tell me what I should or shouldn't do, I'm gonna let you explain yourself."

"Gunshot victims bring cops, for one. Even though I'm sure you've got the locals under control, that was a lot of people that died back there. Innocent people. When the shells from those machine guns are collected, that's gonna bring the feds, and when it comes to them, you always wanna gather your thoughts before answering questions."

Surprisingly, his logic was sound, even though I wanted to argue because I wanted to be by Big's side. The reality was that there was nothing I'd be allowed to do inside this hospital except wait, and Big's instructions weren't to wait, they were to take action.

"I want people watching him in case Rock or Ebony tries to make a move on him at the hospital," I said, climbing back into the truck.

"I can handle that, but our dudes stick out and that ain't good around the feds."

Again, I knew he was right, but there was no way I was leaving Big unguarded.

"I'll take care of it. Just get me to my parent's house," I said, pulling the door closed and grabbing my own phone out of my clutch on the floor.

After a few slow, deep breaths to settle my nerves, I called the chief of police for Fort Worth and informed him that I needed round the clock protection for my man. Of course, he had a million and one questions because he had heard about the shooting, but he didn't get paid to ask questions and I kindly reminded him of that. There was no way to get off the phone though without promising to give him my statement before any other law enforcement agency, so I agreed to be in his office in two hours.

After that call I had no choice except to call the family attorney, Joey Rickard, and let him know what was going on, and he was hell bent on seeing me before we took a meeting with the chief. I knew this would be an exercise in getting my story straight because I was only to say what needed to be said. As we pulled up in front of what was now my house, I didn't know whether to be infuriated that my time to grieve was so grossly interrupted, or thankful to have that pain take a backseat to the rage that was brewing. One thing I knew for sure was that Ebony had no idea what she'd done, and she wouldn't until I was standing over her cold, lifeless body. Her father had gotten off easy, but she wouldn't.

"I want Ebony's house hit, and her parent's house in Houston too," I said.

"But Ivy - "

"No buts, no bullshit. I want everywhere that bitch can hide erased from the earth today! I don't give a fuck if she's on the University of Texas campus, destroy that mu'fucka too!" I yelled, getting out of the truck before he could say anything that was gonna further piss me off.

Once I was inside I went straight upstairs and turned the shower on, stripping my clothes off with my eyes closed so I didn't have to see Big's blood. For an hour I scrubbed and scrubbed, needing to cleanse my body and hands not just of the blood on them now, but the blood that would be there in the future. I could feel the tears on my cheeks, but I no longer knew if they were grief, anger, or acceptance of the loss for what had been my life before now.

College class and exams seemed so far away that they could probably be on Mars, but there was nothing I could do about that. There was no going back, so whatever the future held, I had to embrace it. When I finally turned off the shower I had something like a plan in mind, and that felt better than simply reacting to the chaos. Once I was dressed I went downstairs to my dad's office and made a necessary call to the leader of the Gulf Cartel.

"Manuel, it's me. Did you receive the $3 million?"

"Sí, and your next metric ton of cocaine will be delivered on schedule," he replied.

"Gracias. How would you like to make $5 million more?"

"I'm listening," he replied after a moment's hesitation.

I quickly told him what I needed, knowing it would appeal to him because of mutual interests. By the end of our conversation, I knew that if we pulled this shit off we would control the south together, with bodies stacked high enough to build the president's wall.

CHAPTER 15
EBONY
One month later…

"…In a developing news story straight from the White House, it seems that President Trump will travel to Houston, Texas this week in a show of force for the crackdown on opioid use. As you know in the past month, the number of heroin-related overdoses has quadrupled in number, claiming nearly 100 victims in the month of February alone. It is believed that the heroin overdoses are not simply a byproduct of the ever-growing opioid epidemic, but a bad batch and lethal mixture of the chemicals used to cook it. Given the rising tensions between the warring cartels and the street gangs, it's anyone's guess who's responsible at this point. Today the president made it clear that even if it takes the National Guard, this senseless tragedy must be stopped. He is also now privately raising money to fund the new wall to be built between Mexico and the United States, hoping to have it done within the next twelve months.

"In local news, the FBI and ATF are still in Fort Worth and Houston investigating the massacre that took place at a funeral last month and the subsequent disappearance of business partners Soloman Black and Jacob Dahl. The gravesite service was being held for the wife of Mr. Black, and - "

"Turn that shit off," my mom ordered, sitting on the couch beside me.

"You were the one always telling me to watch the news."

"Yeah, well, that was before our life became part of it in a negative way, and your ass was contributing to that," she replied, twisting the cap off of a mixture bottle of Jack Daniels and draining the contents in two swallows.

It was on the tip of my tongue to make a smart remark about her actions, but it was clear she was already in a bad mood.

"Mom, I didn't start this. I - "

"I don't give a fuck who started it, Ebony! You're involved, and you're gonna end up just like your father!" she yelled, pointing her finger in my face.

"My father is the reason I'm doing all this! Do you not see that? Or am I just supposed to let this bitch get away with what she did?"

"I understand how this started - even if I don't agree with it, I understand. But it's gone too far now, Ebony. Can't you see that?" she asked in a gentler tone.

I wanted to tell her I could definitely see that, but there was so much she still didn't know. I wanted this whole situation to magically go away, or better yet, to have never happened. But those wishes belonged to a naïve college kid that no longer existed. Part of me died that day at Ivy's mom's funeral, and I hadn't prepared myself for that to happen.

I was fueled by so much hate that I actually believed that any life I took was worth it just to get to that bitch, but after that day, I learned how wrong I was. No matter how many sleepless nights I had after that, how many daytime nightmares of watching bodies drop or explode by my hand, I realized some things can't be undone. The saddest part was that now I had no choice except to push forward or risk drowning in what I'd already done.

"Did you ever wonder why Dad never walked away? Why he never just said, fuck it, I've had enough? I used to ask myself that sometimes because I knew it wasn't the money that made him do it. I understand now, though, that a major part of his commitment to that lifestyle was about his thirst and need for power. The other part is because once you're in, there really is no out with these people."

"But you're not involved like your father was, so that's no excuse," she said, opening another mini bottle of liquor and guzzling it.

With the way she was already drinking I wasn't sure how much I should tell her, but I desperately needed to unload the burden I was carrying.

"There's some things I need to tell you, and I need you to listen without judging me," I said.

The look she leveled at me said that might not be possible, but I decided to push on anyway.

"At Margarita's funeral - "

"Stop right there. I don't wanna know shit about that," she said, putting her hand up like I had a gun on her.

She may not have known that I actually pulled the trigger, but the fact that she wouldn't look me in the eye told me she had no doubts I was involved. And she didn't approve.

"After that, I decided to make a more calculated move against Ivy. I knew she's basically taken over our family's business, the legal and illegal for Soloman and the illegal for dad, and I decided she couldn't have it all. Rock made the introductions and I agreed to push product for - "

"Bitch, you what?" she roared, swinging a backhand at me that I just barely escaped.

"Mom, just listen!" I pleaded, scrambling to the other side of the couch.

I could see the fire in her eyes, but she didn't take another swing at me so I took that as a sign to continue.

"Ivy took everything from me, from us, and even after the funeral she kept taking. Both of our houses were destroyed by fire, and now we're forced to call the fucking Marriot home. I just needed to take something from her," I explained passionately.

In my mind I could still feel myself jolted awake by the taste of smoke in my throat right before the smoke detectors started screaming. I could feel the blind panic trying to drown me as I fought to clear my mind and find a way to escape the growing inferno. I thought death was certain, but I managed to stumble down the stairs and outside before the fire could feast on me. A blessing, no doubt, but I still had to watch in horror as that living, breathing thing gave thanks to the night sky by destroying everything I owned, tarnishing the memories that came with those things as well. My mom had experienced the same thing, so how could she not understand my motivation in this moment?

"So why not come to me so we could go after the legit businesses?" my mom asked.

"Because that's not what our fathers died for, so that won't mean as much. Plus, Soloman was smart and so is Ivy, which means there's nothing funny about any legal business. My plan was to crumble her business by getting the same quality product and dropping the price on it until she'd have to either give it away or find another hustle."

"Oh God, I think I see where this is going," she groaned, reaching for another bottle of liquor.

"I can't prove that she had a bad batch of dope sent to my people, but the people I'm in business with assure me it wasn't them because they don't deal with heroin. We've tried to reverse what's happened by flooding the streets with coke, but…people are still dying," I said, feeling sick to my stomach.

"Ebony, you've gotta stop the madness. I mean, are you fucking listening to yourself? You're not a killer, you're not a goddamn drug dealer or the leader of some secret society!

You're a smart girl who's gonna make a difference in the world in a positive way. You've gotta stop this."

"Mom, you can't just walk away from these people."

"Yes, the fuck you can, or better yet, you can fly away! Don't act like I don't have the money and resources to get you out of here and keep you safe," she stated, becoming more animated with each passing minute.

"I can't leave. I can't leave Rock."

"If you make this conversation about some motherfucker who doesn't care enough about you to keep you out of harm's way, I'll beat your ass!" she warned, jumping to her feet.

It was evident that this conversation was beyond the point of rationale or understanding, but I'd started it with the intentions of telling the truth, and it was too late to go back now.

"I'm pregnant," I said softly.

With the way her mouth hung open and her sudden need to take a seat, you would've thought I'd screamed the news at her.

"Y-you're what?" she asked slowly.

"I'm pregnant. About five or six weeks, I guess."

"But you're on birth control, and you're careful, you're always so careful," she said, her shock evident in every word spoken.

"Obviously I've been distracted. I've taken ten different pregnancy tests in the last two days and they all came out the same. I'm pregnant," I repeated, hoping it would sink in for us both. For five solid minutes neither of us spoke. We simply sat on opposite ends of the couch looking at each other. "Mom, say something."

"Who's the father?" she asked.

"Really? So not only am I a drug dealing piece of shit, I'm a hoe now too?"

"I never said you were the first one, and given your sudden lifestyle change, I think asking who the father is happens to be a fair question," she replied calmly.

"Well, sorry to disappoint you, but I ain't fucking a bunch of niggas. Rockafella is the baby's father."

"Does he know?" she asked

"There's too much going on to drop this on him right now."

"Good. I know of an excellent clinic, and - "

"I'm not having a fucking abortion, if that's what you're suggesting," I said heatedly.

"You're twenty-three years old and you somehow think you're the female version of El Chapo. You have no business bringing a baby into the world."

"I'm not killing my baby!" I said, slower and louder so she could hear me.

"Okay, so tell me your plan. You gonna give birth in the stash house or in federal prison? If you're in the stash house, make sure not to confuse the baby formula with a bad batch of heroin or a good batch of coke," she said sarcastically.

It was on the tip of my tongue to say "fuck you" to her, but somehow, I knew that would likely result in me miscarrying from the ass whooping she handed me. My only sane option was to get up and walk out of the room, so that's what I did, thankful that my mother had decided to rent out the whole top floor of the Marriot.

The room I shared with Rock was at the far end of the hall for privacy purposes, and right now I was glad because it felt like anywhere in Texas was too close to Marissa Dahl. Before I used the keycard to enter our room, I took a couple deep breaths to settle both my nerves and my stomach. Once I had my shit together I opened the door to find Rock sitting on the couch with an iPad in his hands.

"What are you doing, bae?" I asked, hoping my voice sounded normal.

"Working."

"On?" I asked, coming over to sit by him.

"Give me a little room, damn," he said irritably, moving away from me.

"What the fuck is your problem?"

"Nothing; I'm straight. I mean, aside from the fact that I'm literally having to give away millions of dollars of coke, and my niggas can't even do that without getting locked up because shit is so hot."

"I'm sorry, I didn't mean to - "

"Bae, I'm not blaming you. Come here," he said, putting the iPad down and pulling me close to him.

It felt good to be in his arms, not in a sexual way, but because here was the only place I felt safe.

"I hate that bitch," he said, clearly frustrated.

I didn't have to ask who he was talking about because the feeling was definitely mutual.

"How do we fix this?"

"I don't know yet, but we've been summoned for a meeting with José," he replied.

I hadn't been in this game as long as Rock or my father, but I knew enough to know that the connect didn't come out unless there was a problem.

"He wants to see both of us?" I asked.

"Of course. As far as he's concerned it's Jacob's daughter that's in complete control, and I'm just the street nigga behind you."

We both know that wasn't true because we were partners in everything, plus Rock was my mentor in all this. José thinking I was destined to be the next boss had worked in my favor - until now, it seemed.

"What does he want?" I asked.

"He probably wants to know what our next move is because we can't make real money under these conditions."

"We don't even know our next move. Shit, we've been playing defense for the last month," I said, leaning back so I could look him in the eye.

"Well, we've gotta plan or next move before 8 a.m. tomorrow because defense don't win this game at this point."

As harsh as his words sounded to my ears, they still rang truth. The first thing Rock had taught me was that this was a world of kill or be killed I was entering, and I need not bullshit myself about that. The only problem was that I had more than just my life to consider now.

"Hey, what's wrong? Why are you crying?" he asked, concerned.

I hadn't planned to tell him about the baby because he had enough to worry about, and now I was questioning whether his response would be the same as my mother's. There was only one way to find out though.

"I h-have to tell you something important, but I don't know how you're gonna react," I said slowly, fighting to hold back my tears.

"Come on, bae, you know that you can talk to me about anything. Tell me what's going on."

"I'm pregnant," I said quickly.

The expression on his face went from concerned to bug-eyed disbelief in seconds, and then I finally saw the shock set in.

"Pregnant," he echoed.

"Yes, and before you say some really dumb shit, the baby is yours."

"Why would I question that? I know you ain't fucking around on me," he stated confidently.

"Yeah, well, my mom doesn't know that because - "

"Oooh, you told your mom? How did that go?" he asked sympathetically.

"I don't wanna talk about that. I wanna know how you feel."

"I feel…I don't know. I'm not mad, if that's what you're wondering. The timing is crazy, but it is what it is, so I guess I'm gonna be a dad," he said calmly.

"So, you want me to have the baby?"

"Bitch, I'll beat you up if you're suggesting what I think you are," he said, quickly getting heated.

"I'm not suggesting it. You know what? Just forget it. What are we gonna do?"

"We got months to figure that out, so right now we need to focus on our more immediate problems. I might have an idea, but it's gonna get ugly," he warned.

"It already is ugly, but death is uglier."

CHAPTER 16
IVY

"No, Destiny, I don't care who it is or how much money they're offering, we're not renting out the restaurant to one couple. Other people made reservations, and to cancel on them says we're putting money before good service. That stops repeat business and costs us in the long run. Figure out another solution to appease all parties and call me back," I said, hanging up.

My father had built or bought into many legit, lucrative businesses all around the world, but he'd never let on how hard it was to manage all of their problems. Despite being in the middle of an ongoing war, I knew it was important to not only keep up the appearance of good business, but to actually do good business, because there was no other way to keep the money clean.

At first, I'd thought about stepping away from some of the obligations, but I knew that wasn't what my dad would have done. The one good thing about his life as a businessman was that he knew how to delegate and put people in the right position. Once I'd made sure no one's hands were in the cookie jar, from the legal or illegal money, I more or less let the businesses run themselves. On days like today when I had important meetings scheduled, it was frustrating dealing with the minor issues, but since I was still on the job training, I had to handle any and everything that came my way.

Thankfully, I hadn't had to actually go to the restaurant in Grand Prairie because the meeting I was preparing for at the Laredo Port Authority was my top priority. It took Big reporting how important this meeting was to actually get me to leave the house because I honestly never wanted to leave his side. That man was literally my everything, and after he'd gotten shot, I made sure he knew that every single day. I knew he loved me too, and not just because he'd saved my life, but because he'd dealt with me hovering over him every day since he got released from the hospital. Thinking about him had me texting him rapidly, talking that talk that I knew would have him ready to dick me down as soon as I walked through the door.

"They're here," Marcus said, sticking his head in the door before showing Jeremy, Roger, and Louis in.

"Gentlemen," I said, standing and smoothing out any wrinkles in the all-white silk shirt and pants set I had on.

"Ivy, it's good to see you," Louis said, extending his hand first.

After we all exchanged pleasantries, we took our seats to get down to business.

"I see the president is coming to town," Roger said.

"He is. There's a bad drug problem in Houston," I replied, suppressing a smile.

"This is causing more blow back than you anticipated, is it not?" Louis asked.

"To tell you the truth, I'd expected a reaction sooner, and I'd expected it to be worse given today's climate on both prescription and illegal drugs. It's still having the desired affect though," I replied.

"Are you sure about that?" Roger asked.

"Was your money not sent to where you specified?" I countered.

"It was, but we need to make sure that everyone who needs to be paid is paid because - "

"Gentlemen, something my father taught me a long time ago is not to count another man's money. I understand that I'm still fairly new to this, but as long as your pockets are straight, let me worry about everybody else," I said calmly, but with enough of an edge to suggest that a change of topic was probably appropriate.

"Are we letting in any more bogus deliveries from the Sinaloa Cartel?" Jeremy asked.

"No, that was a one shot deal to eliminate the competition. We can't risk drawing heat on either of our ports with good or bad drugs right now, so we'll just stick with the electronics until the heat is off," I said.

"Should I keep routing all drugs to the east and west coasts?" Jeremy asked.

"Yeah, they're doing excellent business, which will be reflected in the bonuses you receive," I replied, smiling.

"Bonuses for what? You made all the right connections," Louis said.

"Doesn't matter. We're in this together," I declared, knowing this is exactly how my dad would've done it. Treating people fairly inspired loyalty better than tyranny, and that's how he'd had such a successful run.

"Thank you in advance. By the way, Big's gift is being offloaded as we speak," Louis said.

Hearing this made my smile grow wider because I knew Big would love the car I'd gotten him as soon as he saw it. I knew he could afford his own whip, but he would never drop $1.5 million on a custom cotton and candy blue 2018 Rolls Royce phantom. Fully armored and fully loaded.

"Thank you for securing that for me, and - "

I was interrupted by my phone vibrating on the table. When I looked at the screen, I saw that it was my lawyer calling, which was odd because I'd just see him yesterday when he'd come to update me about the joint agency investigations surrounding my dad's disappearance. So far, the only foul play they suspected was on the part of those who had him because to the trained eye, he was a squeaky clean businessman. Of course, this meant I was under surveillance, and my phone at home was tapped by my approval, but like my lawyer said, if you know they're watching and still get caught, you deserved it.

"Do you need to take that?" Roger asked.

"Nah, it's just my lawyer, but I'll call him back," I replied, sending the call to voicemail.

"I wanted to get all of your opinions on another business venture that Big and I discussed."

Again, my phone going off interrupted me, and again it was my lawyer.

"Joey, I'm in a meeting," I said, answering in annoyance.

"You need to get home," he replied.

"Why, what's wrong?" I asked, feeling my stomach rush to my pedicured feet.

"The cops are out front and Big is barricaded inside. Get home," he ordered, hanging up.

For a moment I could only sit there, completely dumbfounded by what I'd heard because the shit didn't sound real.

"Everything okay?" Louis asked.

"No. I gotta go," I said, grabbing my purse and walking out of the office without a backwards glance.

"Where are - "

"No questions. Take me home," I instructed Marcus, getting into the back of my dad's truck.

Before he could close the door behind me, I was already texting Big as fast as my shaking fingers would allow, asking him what the fuck was going on.

"What's wrong?" Marcus asked once he was behind the wheel and leaving rubber in the parking lot.

I started to scream at him to mind his goddamn business and be the bodyguard/driver Big intended, but then I realized he had a right to know because this was his cousin.

"I just got a call saying Big is barricaded in the house, surrounded by cops, and I don't know why."

He didn't ask any more questions, just pressed harder on the gas pedal like he was trying to put wings on the side of the truck. Two hours later we crept into my parents' neighborhood, which was literally crawling with cops and SWAT team members.

"He still ain't answering your calls or texts?" Marcus asked, pulling to a stop behind the last cop car.

"No," I replied, fighting the terror in my chest from rising any further.

I'd texted and called Big's phone until my fingers hurt, but he wouldn't answer me. I wouldn't call the house for obvious reasons, so I finally didn't have a choice except to call the police chief himself. I didn't wanna make that call because it felt like I'd been using too many favors and resources lately, but I had to know what was going on. And it was worse than I could've imagined.

"What did Hoover Slim say?" I asked.

"He's looking for information on who the witness is to the cold case they want Big for, and he's reaching out to Gangsta Bit to see if Rock is behind this somehow."

"Who's Gangsta Bit?" I asked, watching all the activity swirling around us.

"He runs Global Gangsta. He founded it, but he used to be a Hoover."

"Maybe he can put a stop to - "

"Not likely. He hates Hoovers now," he said, dashing my hopes.

"I've known Rockafella for years and it ain't in him to get the cops involved," I said, thinking out loud.

"True, but as a strategy of war, I could see him manipulating the situation to happen."

I couldn't really argue with that because what little I knew about was I'd learned on the fly. I sent the chief a text message letting him know I was here and where I was waiting. A couple minutes later he opened the back door to my truck and climbed in.

"Step out," I said, locking eyes with Marcus in the rearview mirror.

"It's gonna look weird if we stay in here too long," Chief Stringer said once we were alone.

"I know. Tell me what I can do to make this go way."

"Ivy, that's not possible. You know I owe your family a great debt, and I'm always willing to help, but you see this circus here. It's out of my control," he replied regretfully.

"Didn't you say this shit happened almost three years ago? They should need something more than just some bitch's word about who killed this guy."

"It's eyewitness testimony because she's saying that she was there. She provided details all the way down to how dude's body dropped once he was shot, and let's not forget that the guy in question worked for immigration and customs enforcement," he said.

"So this bitch just happened to be in the desert in El Paso when this allegedly happened? I don't buy that and neither do you."

"I don't know one way or the other, but she's an illegal and claims she was crossing into the U.S. when this happened."

"I bet the bitch wants asylum for her testimony too, right?" I asked, disgusted.

"Actually, no. After she testifies, she'll be deported back to Mexico, and she's agreed to that."

From the sound of things, whoever had set Big up to take this fall had thought of everything, which meant I was in real danger of losing my man. The thought briefly crossed my mind to say fuck it and just band it out with all the law here, some real *Set It Off* type shit. There was no gun for either of us that way though.

"Look, I'ma go inside and get him to come out, but I need you to make a personal call to whoever the magistrate is and get bail approved," I said.

"Bail, on the murder of a law enforcement agent? You must be joking. And he's going in front of a federal judge, not some side county mu'fucka we have in our pocket, Ivy."

"So what the fuck am I supposed to do, let Big go to jail?" I asked, becoming more frustrated.

"I don't know what else you can do, and I don't think I wanna know. I'll get you inside though," he said, opening the truck door and stepping out.

My father had amassed a lot of favors and made valuable contacts in his line of work, but I had no idea where to begin looking for the type of help we needed. I sent my lawyer a text letting him know what was going on and asking his advice. Five minutes later Stringer messaged me saying I had ten minutes to get inside and end this shit before SWAT breached my parents' house. Ten minutes was no time, especially when trying to convince a man to allow himself to go to jail for something serious. After all, we were in Texas, and a conviction meant the death penalty without question. I didn't have a moment to waste second guessing myself though, so I got out of the truck and made my way through the crowd.

"Ma'am, you can't go - "

"It's okay, she's the owner of the house," Chief Stringer said, taking me by the arm and escorting me past the rest of the cops. "You gotta make this quick, Ivy. The SWAT team is anxious because this has been going on for a couple hours. They would've been in there already, but there are a lot of weapons registered to this address," he whispered, handing me a bullhorn.

"Babe, I'm coming in by myself," I announced with the bullhorn, passing it back and making a beeline for the front door.

I didn't bother with my house key, but instead used the palm scanner so he would know it was me and not shoot.

"Big, where are you?" I yelled, quickly closing the door behind me.

To my left a light came on in the living room, revealing him and the arsenal he had laid out on the coffee table and couch.

"Babe," I said, rushing into his arms and holding him tightly.

"Ivy, I didn't do this. I've done a lot of shit, but this body ain't mine, I promise."

"Do you know who did it?" I asked, pulling back to look up into his face.

The red lines of stress were prominently standing out in the whites of his eyes and I could smell liquor on his breath, but I didn't think he was drunk.

"Yeah, I know who did it. I was there when the shit went down."

"Okay, so - "

"Don't suggest that I tell, because you know I don't get down like that, babe," he stated immediately.

"I wasn't gonna say nothing like that. I was gonna tell you about Hoover Slim going to Gangsta Bit to see what he could find out, because somebody is trying to put you in a trick bag."

"From the looks of shit outside, they've succeeded. Why did you come, babe? I didn't want you caught up in all this," he said, kissing me on the forehead.

"Don't ask dumb questions. We don't have time for that right now. You gonna turn yourself in and - "

"Whoa, you buggin'," he said, stepping back until my arms were no longer around him.

"I'm buggin'? Nigga, if you think you're gonna kill a bunch of cops and survive, then you're fucking buggin'!" I said angrily.

"I'm not 'bout to go to jail for this shit. A conviction would mean - "

"I know what a conviction would mean, Big, but you don't got no other option except to fight it legally now. I'm already trying to figure out how to get you a bond, and if that happens, then we're out of the country until we can sort this shit out. Right now, you gotta go in, unless you want us both to die," I said, picking up the AR-15 off of the table.

The fight was easy to read in his eyes, but he knew me well enough to know that either way it went I wasn't leaving this house without him.

"We can go out hand in hand, or body bag and body bag. Your choice," I said seriously.

"So you want me to go to jail?"

"No, I want you to live! I'm behind you and I'll always be behind you, so stop acting like I'ma leave you for dead or something," I said, again closing the distance between us until I was looking up into his face.

"I didn't do this, Ivy."

"You said that already and I believed you the first time. We both know who's behind this play, but they're stupid because they're underestimating me by thinking that I can't make the world shake without you. I can and I will. Please just trust me, babe," I pleaded.

It was evident that he still wanted to argue, but instead, he undid the straps on the bulletproof vest he was wearing and pulled it off. Next, he took the AR-15 from my grasp and tossed it on the couch before pulling me tightly against him and kissing me thoroughly. I knew time was of the essence, but nothing else mattered when I was in his arms.

"How long before they come in?" he asked.

"They said ten minutes, but they won't just rush the spot now that I'm in here. We still should hurry," I said, already unbuttoning his pants while he went to work on mine.

In seconds he had me spun around and bent over the couch with his dick deep inside me, feeding me pounding jackhammer strokes.

"This p-pussy is y-yours," I panted, clenching my pussy walls around him with every dive he took inside me.

When I felt his hands go to my ass cheeks and spread them, allowing him to step into his strokes, I came instantly.

"C-cum inside me," I demanded, pumping that ass back at him faster.

"I will," he growled, pounding me savagely.

"Ohhh shit!" I called, hit by an aftershock that led straight into another orgasm.

By the time he finally came in me five minutes later, I'd lost the ability to hold myself up and I was face down screaming my love into the leather couch cushions. Neither of us wanted to stop, but the police weren't known for their patience, especially with black folks.

"So how are we gonna do this?" he asked, pulling me upright so I could fix my clothing.

"I'll walk out first, and you follow behind me with your hands all the way up in the air. You already know I'm following you to the police station."

After a deep breath he nodded his head, and now I could see the worry in his eyes.

"We'll get through this," I said, wrapping my arms around him and squeezing like I never wanted to let go.

We got to stay like that for a full two minutes before my phone started going off, and I didn't have to look to know who it was.

"Come on," I said, taking his hand and leading him slowly outside.

Despite all the commotion, he was taken into custody without incident and without being shot down. On my way to the precinct I got a text from my lawyer saying that a top federal trial lawyer named David Barkley would meet us down there and that he used to be a federal prosecutor, so we were in good hands. I felt slight relief, but I knew we were still facing an uphill battle that would require legal and illegal maneuvering.

"Put the word out: a million dollars cash to whoever snatches Ebony's mom. I know they're hiding in plain sight, and for that type of money, somebody in Houston should be able to make her ass disappear without hesitation," I said to Marcus, hopping out of the truck to enter the police station.

It was a full five hours later before I finally came back out, frustrated and discouraged by the bullshit called the justice system. It would be days before Big had a bail hearing, but he knew no matter how much it was, I would post it.

"Let's go," I said, climbing into the back of the truck. It took me a few seconds to realize Marcus was asleep.

“Wake up and drive,” I said, tapping him on the shoulder.

Instead of doing as I instructed, but his body slumped over into the passenger seat, unresponsive. I knew the prickling feeling on the back of my neck wasn’t any type of breeze blowing, and that immediately had me reaching under the driver’s seat for the pistol grip RAS_47 I kept there. No sooner had my head come back up then I heard the shots coming from my right, bouncing off the armor in the truck. My jumping was involuntary, but I quickly aimed at who was shooting and pulled the trigger, allowing the hot, armor-piercing rounds to make lunch meat of my door. I didn’t let up until I heard tires squealing, but it was too late to run because the cops now had me surrounded.

CHAPTER 17
EBONY

"What happened?" I asked when Rock hung up the phone.

"Shit went according to plan."

"Meaning Big's in jail and she's dead?" I asked, hopeful.

Sure, it would've felt much better to put the bullet in the bitch myself, but like Rock had told me, dead was dead.

"Big is definitely in jail, but so is Ivy."

"Well, we knew that could happen because we knew she'd probably have a gun and fight back," I said, trying to hide my disappointment.

"Right. So now we make our next move and start hijacking all shipments that come in through Laredo or Galveston."

"It'll be hard to get them once they've docked though, babe," I replied.

"Don't worry about that. My niggas is pirates and they hungry, so -"

His ringing phone interrupted our little strategy session, but I decided that while he took his call, I'd get us something to drink to celebrate our victory. It really felt like the first one since all this shit had started, but it would definitely get better from here. At least we now had a plan and direction we could tell José about instead of showing up looking like incompetent assholes.

I decided to skip the mini-bar and order up a bottle of champagne - on my mom's tab, of course. I'd just tell her we were celebrating her future grandchild, which we'd done, multiple times, in multiple positions. Remembering what took place earlier had my coochie throbbing again, so after the bottle arrived, I took off all my clothes and went back into the bedroom.

"How about another round?" I asked seductively.

The look on Rock's face said that sex was definitely off the menu right now.

"What's wrong? Who was on the phone?" I asked.

"Bit."

I'd never actually met Gangsta Bit, but I'd seen him from a distance and that nigga didn't look friendly. He and Rock were closer than peanut butter and jelly though, so I didn't understand the disturbed look on his face.

"Okay, so what did he have to say?" I asked, sitting down at the foot of the bed.

"He wants to meet."

"Did you tell him that we've got to go to Mexico in the morning?"

"He don't wanna meet with you; he wants to meet with me. Tonight," he replied.

The misgivings he was feeling were clear in his voice, but I really didn't understand why.

"What are you not telling me, bae?" I asked, moving around on the bed until we were facing each other.

Ordinarily me sitting with my legs crossed and giving him a clear view of this kitty would be too much for his eyes to resist, but right now he was looking through me. His reaction to this call was starting to scare me, but I waited for him to speak instead of pressing for info.

"Bit and I go way back, back to my days as a Hoover. I was actually with him when he went to the west coast and was sanctioned to start Global Gangsta. I was the first homie to move with the movement, so I knew what it took to get to where we are now. And I know how ruthless Bit is."

"Okay, but you two are friends, more like brothers from what you just described," I said, still not understanding his reaction to being summoned to a meeting.

"Brothers, huh? Yeah, well, that didn't stop Cain from killing Abel."

His statement caused real fear to enter my bloodstream, but I tried not to overreact or show the rising panic I was feeling.

"Y-you think he's gonna kill you?" I asked slowly.

"With Bit you never know until it's too late. I know he's pissed off about something, and if I was a betting man, I'd say it had everything to do with the last move we made."

"But he knows we're at war with this, bitch so - "

"He does, but he doesn't. What I mean is that I've been doing this long enough not to need my hand held when I make a move. We should've had a sit down before now about a full scale war though," he admitted.

"If he's that mad, then don't go right now, bae. Just buy some time because we'll have the upper hand soon."

"It ain't that simple. I can't just not show up because that's the type of disrespect that ain't tolerated. I damn sure wouldn't tolerate it," he replied honestly.

At this point I didn't really give a fuck about the code him and his niggas lived by. I simply wanted my man to survive the storm and come out on the other side with me. And our baby. I knew I couldn't say any of that to him though. I couldn't cry and beg him not to go or come up with some half-assed plan that involved us running away. I had to put my big girl panties on because I was the woman of a Global Gangsta, which meant we took the world on when necessary.

"What do you want me to do, bae?" I asked.

"I want you to mentally prepare for your sit down with José tomorrow because - "

"Wait, what the fuck do you mean my sit down with José? You're going too," I said, fighting to keep all the hysteria bubbling inside me down.

"The plan is for me to go with you, but I might not be back in time because Bit is in L.A. right now, and that's where I have to go. I'll take your dad's plane, and if I'm done before you are, then I'll fly down there. But you don't need me there with you, Ebony."

Everything in me wanted to scream at him just how much I needed him, but again I had to remember my position and the fact that I'd chosen this life.

"When are you leaving?" I asked softly.

"After we celebrate," he replied, taking the bottle from my hands and popping the cork.

"You only get one glass too with your pregnant ass."

"That's all I want. I'll call and get the plane ready for you," I said, getting off the bed and going back into the living room to get my phone out of my pants on the floor.

I could've used his phone, but I wanted a minute to reel in my emotions before I went against what I knew I should do and started begging. I took my time making the necessary calls before grabbing the glasses they'd sent up with the bottle and returning to the room.

"The plane will be ready to leave within the hour," I said handing him the glasses.

"Thank you, bae. Listen, if you want me to I'll call José and set the meeting for a later time."

"No. I'm not gonna show any weakness or make him think I'm unsure of myself in any way. I'ma handle this shit like a boss," I vowed.

"Come here."

I did as instructed, expecting to receive the glass of champagne he'd just poured, but instead he set both the glass and bottle on the nightstand. When I was standing directly in front of him, he put his hands on my waist, giving me chills in a pleasantly familiar way while pulling me closer. His kisses started on my stomach, covering every inch of the flat surface with a love that melted my heart.

When his lips moved up, capturing a nipple on the way, I felt the heat ignite between my legs, letting me know that something else was hot enough to melt. His kisses turned to licks from one nipple to the other, making my knees knock like the boogie man was at the door, and I wanted him to come in. When he stood up I thought my lips would find his, but suddenly his grip on my waist tightened and I was tossed into the air effortlessly.

“Rock!” I screamed, wrapping my arms around his head as he caught me with one of my legs on either shoulder.

I didn’t know if he wanted to talk, but if he did he’d be doing it to my pussy lips because he was face deep. He spun me around, laying me gently on the bed, and only then did the feast begin. In all the time we’d been together he’d never licked my asshole, at least not on purpose. Within seconds that changed as he took a long, lazy taste of me from bottom to top, freezing my breath in my lungs while my eyes lost focus. If I thought his actions were an accident, him sticking his tongue in and out of my asshole put that to rest and sent my body into an unfamiliar frenzy.

“Okay, okay, okay, I’m okayyy,” I sang out, fighting the urge to grab his head tighter.

My vocal outburst let him know I was at his mercy, and that’s when shit got real. Suddenly my ass was only part of the three-ring circus that was my pussy and clit, but I was too open to complain. For what felt like hours he ate me, drank me, and then ate me some more until all I could do was whimper in ecstatic bliss. When he was satisfied with the beautiful torture he’d laid down, he stepped back to admire his handiwork. I knew I looked like a fish out of water or a mermaid trapped on land, but I didn’t give a fuck. With the way he was looking at me, I thought the dick was next, and I didn't know if I could handle that.

"D-don't hurt me," I said, smiling in satisfaction.

"I won't. I just wanted to give you something to hold you until I meet up with you tomorrow.

"Wait, we not gonna - "

"No, bae, but you can come take a shower with me," he said, scooping me up in his arms and carrying me to the bathroom.

I thought he might change his mind once we were both naked, soaping each other down, but his focus was on giving me a sensual bathing. That was the icing on the cake after our bedroom activities, but I was concerned because he wasn't asking for or letting me get him off.

"Bae, what's going on?" I asked while he was drying me off.

"Nothing, I just want you to be as relaxed as possible when you go into that meeting."

"And I want the same for you, so why don't you just let me - "

"Nah, I don't need to be relaxed. I need to be on point," he said seriously.

One thing I'd never do is try to tell him how to do him, so I dropped the conversation. We both dressed in silence, each wrapped up in our own thoughts about the immediate future.

"I'll text you when I land," he promised, kissing me in a way that had me wanting to get naked again.

"I'll be waiting."

I couldn't deny the loneliness I felt once he was gone, but I kept myself busy by planning for my own trip. It was a huge risk to go to Mexico, especially since my passport had been destroyed in the fire, but I had to handle my business. I never got around to my glass of champagne, but I continued my celebration with a hearty meal of steak and potatoes for me and the baby.

Part of me wanted to go down the hall and talk to my mom, but right now it felt like too much space was in between us. Intellectually she may have understood why I was doing shit the way I was doing it, but emotionally she wasn't on the same page with me. I was my father's daughter, and if a mu'fucka had done to me what was done to him, I had no doubts that he would've torched the world from the inside out. So how could I not do the same? I had no choice except to see this shit through because I'd come way too far to go back. If she couldn't understand that, or couldn't love me despite that, then I'd just have to live with my decisions on my own. I'd always have Rock to support me.

I lay in bed tossing and turning, thinking about him until I finally got a text in the middle of the night saying that he'd arrived safely. I thought that would've been enough to let me get some sleep, but two hours later I was still lying in bed looking up at the ceiling, wondering if he was okay. I tried distracting myself by focusing on what I had to do, and that actually allowed me to doze off. Before I knew it, though, the sun was coming through the blinds, forcing me to get out of bed and get on the move. The first thing I did was check my phone for texts, and when I found none, I sent one to Rock immediately asking if he was going to Mexico.

I knew watching my phone wouldn't make him hit back any faster, so I got up and got on with the day. By the time I got to the private airfield where the helicopter was waiting, all I'd heard from Rock was that he couldn't make the meeting, but he knew I could handle it. When I tried to ask about his meeting I got no response, and that worried me more than it pissed me off. Still, I did what he'd expected me to do, and got on the helicopter.

An hour and a half later I touched down in Mexico, stepping out in a bold red form-fitting Michael Kors number with a vintage matching Prada bag that concealed twin Ruger 9mm's. All sexy and all business.

"Nice to see you again, Señorita Dahl," José said, taking my hand and kissing it.

"Likewise. Rock sends his apologies, but he had an engagement that he couldn't get out of."

"I understand, and our business shouldn't take long. Please," he said, stepping aside so I could get to the open door of his waiting SUV.

Once we were loaded up, the three trucks moved out at a high rate of speed. For a moment I questioned if I'd ever step foot back on American soil again, but I had to quickly banish those thoughts because men like José smelled fear like a blood hound.

"I saw on the news that things are not going so well in your part of town," he said, lighting a cigar.

"We're still dealing with the after-effects of the bad dope, but we're handling it. Actually, the tide will be turning in our favor very soon."

"Ah. This is good news. Tell me, does this have anything to do with both Ivy and her boyfriend being in police custody?" he asked.

I had to work extremely hard not to let my surprise show because I had not expected him to know about that move already. Then again, I should've expected it because the cartel was not only connected but invested.

"Yes, this has something to do with that. Their legal troubles mean they're not focused and we've already made plans to take full advantage of that," I said confidently.

"Wars cost money - not just fighting them, but the heat that comes with them that restricts business. In the beginning the ends justified the means, but as time has passed, a lot of money has been lost, and this we cannot accept. So I'm going to give you something to end this once and for all."

"What is it?" I asked eagerly.

His response was to keep puffing on his cigar. Twenty minutes later we pulled up to what appeared to be an abandoned apartment building. Again, the thought of death crossed my mind, but I quickly banished the thought and got out of the truck with José. We followed two of his men into a first floor disaster that used to be an apartment, and I was led to the one bedroom in the back. José paused for a minute to study me, and then he opened the door. I couldn't believe what I was seeing, but I immediately understood it was a game changer.

"She'll come for him wherever, whenever," I said.

"And when she does, you kill them both."

CHAPTER 18
IVY
Four days later…

"Seriously, Joey, four fucking days! What the fuck do I pay you for if it takes four days to get me out of jail for some bullshit?" I asked hastily, walking past him and out of the police station.

"You act like it was a routine traffic stop, Ivy. You killed someone literally in front of the police station, with an assault rifle no less. You're lucky you aren't still sitting in there facing a murder charge like Big."

Hearing this made me stop in my tracks and turn on him fast.

"Watch how you talk to me," I warned in a low growl.

"I'm just saying it wasn't an everyday situation you were involved in. There were questions - a lot of questions - given everything that's been going on with your family. And it wasn't just the locals because the FBI was down here before I was. It's under control now though. You won't be charged with anything because the RAS-47 may look and shoot like the AK-47, but it's American made. You know your dad was smart enough to register the gun he kept in his truck for easy access."

"Yeah, I know. Tell me what the situation is with Big," I said, turning and leading the way down the steps to Big's custom Phantom.

With my dad's truck now in the impound lot, it was the safest vehicle to travel in until I could have changes made to my Aston Martin.

"The bail hearing is tomorrow, and David thinks he has a shot at getting him out, but - "

"But what?" I asked, stopping next to the car.

"You're gonna have to put everything on the line: the businesses, the houses, everything. And if he doesn't show up or if he leaves the country, the government is gonna seize everything without hesitation."

"We can't just put up the money?" I asked, confused.

"If he gets a bond it won't be about the money. It'll be about his ties to the community and the likelihood that he won't run. You putting everything on the line is the only way to demonstrate that, and you might get mad at me for saying this, but I wouldn't advise you to do it."

I know he was speaking as my lawyer who was trying to protect all I had, even if that meant protecting me from myself. That was the only reason I didn't cuss him the fuck out.

"Key?" I asked with my hand open.

Once he'd given me the car key I opened the door and got in, waiting for him to do the same so we could get the fuck out of dodge."

"Did you get to see Big?" I asked once we were on the move.

"Yeah. I didn't want him to hear about what happened from anyone except me. He took the news about his cousin hard, but he was next level pissed when I told him about you. The only way I could calm him down was to promise to make a call for him, so he knew you'd be okay."

"What call? To who?" I asked.

"Well, the dude you killed was a Hoover, so he had me call some guy named Slim to report that and to get you round the clock protection."

"And when is that supposed to start?" I asked, wishing it was Big himself out here to look after me.

Knowing that one of his own had turned on us made me more than a little nervous about trusting anyone right now.

"It started the moment we left the police station. There's at least five trucks following us now," he replied.

Looking in the rearview mirror I saw that he was telling the truth, but I had no doubt there were more goons lurking.

"What else did Big ask you to do?"

"Get him the fuck out," he replied simply.

It hurt me to know that my baby was caged in, but I was gonna do everything in my power to set him free, and if he wanted to run, I would without looking back. Big was all I had, and I'd follow him to the end of the earth.

"Where's your car?" I asked.

"I left it at your parents' house. By the way, your name is officially on it as the owner now, per your mom's will."

I could take no joy in that news because I'd rather have my mother back than anything material in the world, but I would look after everything for as long as I could.

"What did you find out about the whole situation at the police station?" I asked, checking my review mirror again to make sure I hadn't lost the army behind me.

"Marcus took two shots to the chest, obviously with a silencer because no one heard any gunfire until they came for you. Based on the shells found, they believe it was two shooters, but as of yet there's no I.D. on the second one."

I didn't know whether the plan had been to kill me or kidnap me, but it definitely wasn't a coincidence that this happened the moment Big wasn't by my side. I was getting real sick of this bitch Ebony, and her nigga too, so it was time to stop playing games and checkmate that ass.

"I'ma lay low for a while, but I'll be in touch," I said once I'd pulled up in front of my house.

"That's a good idea because the feds are definitely watching, and you're no good to Big if you're dead or in jail your damn self."

"I'll be fine, don't worry," I said.

Despite my words, the look he was giving me said he was gonna do just that. Even though I was grown, I still appreciated his concern because the number of people who actually cared about me in this world was dropping fast. I could tell he wanted to say something, maybe even give me some fatherly advice since he'd seen me grow up, but he held his tongue and got out of the car. I followed his lead, going in the opposite direction so I could get what I needed out of the house. I opened the door with the intention of going to my dad's office, but I pulled up short at the sight of a nigga sitting on my couch. My first thought was to get to the nearest gun, but the fact that I recognized him made me pause.

"Ain't you that rapper from Houston?" I asked.

"To most people, but to those that really know me, I'm Hoover Slim."

"Oh, okay. How the fuck did you get in my house though?" I asked, no longer star-struck.

"I got many talents besides rappin'. I mean you no disrespect or harm though. I'm actually here to make sure you're good after what went down."

"I'm fine. My only concern is getting Big out of jail," I said honestly.

"I'm working on that too, and that's why I gotta get back to Houston ASAP. Are you staying here or coming with me?"

"Neither. I'ma stay in Fort Worth because Big's here, but not in this house because the feds are watching, and I can't have them peeping my moves," I said.

"For a college kid, you're becoming good at thinking like someone from the street."

"That's not condescending at all," I replied sarcastically.

"It wasn't meant to be. I meant it as a compliment. I'ma keep it 100 with you and tell you that I told Big Cuzz I didn't think you had what it took to fill your pops' shoes and that you'd probably get him killed. Glad I was wrong."

Right about now was the time when a nigga would get cursed the fuck out for judging me without knowing me, but I actually understood that in his world judgement and instincts were the difference between life and death.

"Big taught me well," I replied, missing my man more and more with each passing minute.

"You got a plan to get him out?" Slim asked.

"I got a lawyer for that. I got a plan to end this little cat and mouse game that Ebony and Rockafella are playing because I'm sick of it."

"Kick it to me," he said, gesturing towards the green leather loveseat that was directly across from the matching couch he was occupying.

"I guess you're the person I need to talk to anyway," I said, sitting down. "Before all hell broke loose at the police station, I'd asked Marcus to put a $1 million-dollar bounty on Marissa Dahl, Ebony's mom. Marissa is something like a southern socialite, born into money and not familiar with the streets, so I figured she'd be an easy target. From my point of view, she was only safe because she's in Houston, and Global Gangsta controls that area, but $1 million is a lot of money for the average mu'fucka."

"True. You seem to be confused on some things though. Global doesn't control Houston. We share it, and there ain't been much of that since this war started. The Hoovers are gonna back Big Cuzz no matter what but we're still about our money, which is why both me and Gangsta Bit have tried to remain on the sideline. Given everything that's happened, we had to have a sit down," he informed me.

"Okay," I replied slowly, evaluating him and trying to see where this was going.

"I can't tell you all that was said, but what it comes down to is that this shit is hurting his business, and he's unhappy. Our business is growing, however, which means he had to bring something to the table to negotiate a truce with," he said, sailing.

"Who are you to call a truce for me when this situation doesn't really concern you?" I asked, becoming pissed.

"I understand that this ain't business for you, it's personal, and I respect that. But what you need to understand is that anything involving Big concerns me. The reason that I liked your pops was because he understood that he's gotten to a point where he couldn't be in the street anymore, but he never forgot the value of a street nigga. Do you understand that?" he asked.

There was a smart-ass retort on the tip of my tongue begging for me to let it fly, but I did understand the threat that was given in warning. No matter who I'd killed or what I'd done up to this point, I was still a spoiled little rich girl to the niggas who did the real dirty work on a daily basis. I had too much to lose to act like I didn't, which meant I would need dudes like Hoover Slim.

"I understand, and you're right, this is personal for me. I didn't have a problem with Global Gangsta as a whole, but after what was done to my father and at my mom's funeral, this can't end until she's dead," I said honestly.

For a moment he simply stared at me, and then he gave me a lazy smile.

"Believe it or not, I anticipated that being your answer, so I secured a few things to help you out with that."

His response made me raise a quizzical eyebrow and look around the room, but I didn't spot anything out of the ordinary.

"Come on, take a ride with me," he said, standing.

"I need to wash that funky-ass jail off me first."

"That's cool. I'll be out front," he said, leaving me alone.

I was curious as to what he had in mind that would result in that bitch Ebony's head mounted on my wall like a hunting trophy, knowing that the sooner I finished up here, the sooner I'd find out. I put a little pep in my step as I got up and went upstairs. I really wanted to take a long bubble bath, but I settled for a blistering hot fifteen minute shower for now. Once that was done I threw on a pair of black Polo jeans with the matching turtleneck and grabbed two bags to put the shit in that I would need. After I had my clothes packed I took the other bag to my dad's office where the gun safe was, getting a different Glock, a sawed-off 20 gauge, and plenty of ammo. With everything I needed, I went outside and loaded the car.

"That's a nice ride," Slim commented.

"It's Big's."

"Damn, he ain't tell me he had this. Maybe I should - "

"He doesn't know he has this, and no you shouldn't," I said, shooting down any idea he had about driving or borrowing my man's car. He had enough money to buy his own.

"You can follow me then," he said, climbing into the back of one of the range rovers that had escorted me from the police station.

I had no idea where we were going, but I got behind him as he pulled off and the other four trucks got behind me. Two hours later I was shocked to find myself pulling up to my own townhouse.

"What are we doing here?" I asked once I was out of the car.

"Don't worry. According to my people, your spot ain't under surveillance because you ain't been here in a long while. After you," he said, stepping aside so I could lead the way inside.

Unlike at my other house, four of Slim's people followed us in, which made me a little nervous until I spotted the present he'd left on my living room floor.

"My birthday isn't for months," I said, looking at Slim and smiling.

"I'm early, but it's okay, right?"

In the middle of my living room, laid out on plastic, were a very naked Rock and Marissa, bound and gagged. Ebony was all that was missing, but having these two meant I'd have her soon.

CHAPTER 19
EBONY

I'd never needed a drink so bad in my entire life! I felt like I was losing my fucking mind, and there was no hope of regaining it without a fifth of something potent to sooth me. The baby growing inside me was all that kept the bottle of Hennessy on the table in front of me unopened. If I was honest with myself, though, I didn't know how much longer the baby could be my strength. I needed Rockafella. I hadn't heard a single word from him in four days, and the GPS on his phone had him still in L.A. I didn't wanna assume the worst, but it was unlike him to disappear without telling me something, and there was no way he'd do that now with me being pregnant.

My heart couldn't accept that he was dead. I felt deep down I would know because he was my soulmate, and no one could lose that without feeling something. So, where was he? Where the fuck was my man? I'd asked myself that one question so many times, going from angry to devastated so much that I felt truly crazy. And to top it all off, my mom was off doing her thing so I couldn't even go to her for support or a shoulder to cry on! I'd never felt more alone in my life, and I had absolutely no fucking idea what to do about it. The sound of my phone binging startled me so bad that I knocked it off the table trying to grab it.

"Rock?" I said by way of answering, praying to hear my baby's voice.

"Sorry, it's just me."

"I-Ivy?" I asked, in disbelief at the nerve of this bitch.

"'Sup, sis? I just called check on you, you know, see how you were doing."

"Bitch, fuck you!" I yelled, hanging up on her.

In this moment I didn't know what I wanted more: her dead or Rock to walk through the hotel room door. To my amazement, my phone started ringing again, and when I looked at the screen, I saw that the call was coming from a private number. After about seven rings it became clear to me that whoever was calling was intent on speaking to me, and since it could be Rock, I had to answer.

"Hello?" I answered cautiously.

"It's not polite to hang up on people, EB. I thought we were better than that."

"Yo, bitch, you've got some nerve! We ain't better than shit, and as soon as I get the chance, I'ma cut your fucking heart out! You call me again and you'll regret it," I promised, once again hanging up on her.

Right about now I was wishing I'd taken José up on his offer, but like a dummy, I'd put off the decision until I could strategize with Rock. The bottom line was that I had to deal with this bitch, and fast. This time when my phone went off it wasn't a call, but a text. A picture was downloading and when it finally came through, I dropped my phone, refusing to believe what my eyes were telling me. My tears were instantaneous, and I could feel all the food I'd eaten during these four days of depression wanting to come back up.

My phone was ringing again, but I couldn't pick it up because then I'd have to look at the picture and know that this shit was real. Grabbing the bottle of liquor off the table in front of me, I quickly unscrewed the top and had it halfway to my mouth before I pulled back and launched it at the wall. Hearing and seeing it shatter made me feel a little better, but as soon as my phone started ringing again, I was right back in hell. Every fiber of my being was screaming at me not to answer, but I knew I didn't really have a choice, so I reluctantly picked the phone up.

"You're evil," I said, trying to hold my tears in so I wouldn't give this bitch the satisfaction.

"I'm no more evil than your father made me, sis, so if you wanna blame, somebody blame him. Although it's bad manners to speak ill of the dead."

The sound of her voice had the bile rising in my throat, forcing me to choke it down because I refused to let this bitch know how bad she'd hurt me.

"What…do…you…want?" I growled through clenched teeth.

"A simple trade will suffice. You can take your mom's place."

"And what about Rock?" I asked, heartbroken.

"I think it's poetic that you two die together, don't you think? Or I can just send you pictures of him and your mom after their souls have left their bodies. Maybe I'll even send you their bodies back…one piece at a time, of course."

There were so many words I wanted to spew at her, so many names I wanted to call her, but when I opened my mouth, only vomit came flying out. I'd never been so mad as I was at this moment and I couldn't hold it in anymore.

"Sounds like you're a little under the weather," she said, laughing.

I pulled the phone away from my ear long enough to take a few deep breaths and wipe my mouth, knowing I needed to get this over with.

"Where do you wanna meet?" I asked finally

"Let's meet somewhere you're familiar with. How about where your parent's house used to be? I'm sure the previous tenants won't mind."

"When?" I asked.

"Be there at midnight."

I didn't say shit else. I hung up and ran to the bathroom where I threw up violently again. After ten minutes of hugging the toilet bowl I was finally able to get up and splash some cold water on my face. I didn't have to look in the mirror to know that death was written all over my face, I could feel it with every beat of my heart. I knew my mother wouldn't want me to sacrifice my life for hers, but it was my fault that she was in this situation.

Even now I could hear her words telling me that this shit had gone too far, but I hadn't listened, and now it was time to pay for it. Or was it? I still had one move left and thinking about this sent me running from the bathroom in search of my phone. The smell of throw up was real in the living room from where I'd vomited on the floor, and it was threatening to make me do it again. Still, I fought threw it long enough to get my phone and go out on the balcony. I had to take a few moments for my hands to stop shaking so I could dial the number, but once I finally got it done it was answered immediately.

"Buenos tardes, Señorita Dahl. How are you today?" José asked.

I had a moment of indecision about how to play this, but I knew not to bullshit him because he had eyes everywhere.

"I got a situation out here, but it will turn out beneficial to the overall plan we discussed a few days ago."

"What is it you need from me?" he asked.

"I need a recent picture, and I need to know if you can get here tonight for the meeting."

"Tonight? That is really short notice."

"I know, but if I don't handle this tonight, somebody else I love is gonna die. Can you get him here by midnight?" I asked, preparing to beg if I needed to.

In the silence that followed I could hear José thinking, although I didn't know what the holdup was about considering the speech he'd gave the other day.

"The picture should be coming to your phone now. Where is the meeting place?" he asked.

"The land that use to be my parents' house."

"We will be there," he promised, hanging up.

For the first time in four days I sighed in relief, knowing that the game wasn't lost just yet. It was time for that bitch to get a taste of her own medicine. After the picture I asked for downloaded to my phone, I shot it straight to the number that had texted the photos to me. I didn't have to wait long for my phone to start ringing instantly, but I decided to send it to voicemail because I wanted that bitch to drown in her feelings. It was no surprise when the phone started ringing again, but I ignored it and went about the business of calling housekeeping to clean up my mess.

Despite the photo, I knew Ivy would still feel like she had an advantage because it was obvious Big's people were still behind him, and Global had betrayed Rock. She wasn't counting on José coming to my rescue though, but she would quickly learn that the enemy of my enemy was always a friend. I let her continue calling for a full thirty minutes before I decided to answer.

"What's up, sis?" I asked.

"Don't play with me, bitch! Where the fuck is my father?" I could hear the tears through the thickness in her voice, and that made me smile.

"You wanna know where he's at, or where he's gonna be?" I asked, taunting her.

"Let's not play games, Ebony. I've got what you want, and you've got what I want."

"Playing games was so fun for you a minute ago, sis, but now that the rabbit has the gun, you wanna get serious. Doesn't seem fair," I said.

"Bitch, just give me my father!" she roared, clearly not liking my teasing tone.

"Calm down, bitch, I'ma give him to you. We do the exchange tonight like we agreed, and since I don't have an army, you better not bring another soul with you or I'ma dead that nigga while you watch," I promised, hanging up.

I had a lot of hours between now and when the exchange went down to come up with an exit strategy because I knew there was no way Ivy would come by herself. I quickly sent José a text, asking him to move some of his men onto the property immediately before Ivy did it. That still didn't level the playing field because she had the Hoovers, Global Gangsta, and the Gulf Cartel behind her, but having something was better than nothing. For a brief moment it actually crossed my mind to call the police, but it wasn't a part of the world that could do that anymore. I had to view law enforcement as the opposition.

"We're gonna get through this," I said, sitting on the bed and rubbing my stomach.

Some would say that I wasn't far enough along to consider my little one a baby, but their opinion didn't matter. My baby and its father were my world, and now it was my job to protect them both. I needed more insurance, and at this point I could only think of one person to call. I almost hung up after the continuous ringing went unanswered, but finally I heard his voice.

"Hey, J, it's been a long time," I said hesitantly, not really knowing what to expect.

"Ebony, is that you?"

"Yeah, it's me, and I need your help," I replied honestly.

"Tell me what's going on."

Even though he hadn't agreed to help, I still felt some relief just at the fact that he hadn't hung up on me yet. Justice was someone from my past that I never could or would forget, but there was a certain way you held a nigga down while he was doing time, and I'd failed. Still, when he'd gotten out a year ago he'd hit me up on Facebook to say hi, and he slid in my DM from time to time to check on me. We were friends, but the friendship was hard to maintain because of his affiliations with the enemies of Global Gangstas.

All that shit didn't matter anymore. I didn't waste time with small talk. Instead, I ran down the last few months of my life and the drastic changes that had occurred. I didn't throw a pity party. I just laid out the facts, even though I knew he'd feel sympathy for me. I needed his help more than sympathy.

"What do you need?" he asked once I'd finished running it down.

"I need you to have my back. You're the only person I can trust."

"You don't gotta ask twice. I can't even imagine Ivy getting down like that," he said, disbelief coating his words.

"A lot has changed. We've changed."

"Yeah, but you shouldn't have. This life ain't for either of you because it'll turn you into someone you can't even face in the mirror. It'll make you hate yourself as much as you do your enemy," he said.

I knew all too well the truth in what he was speaking on, just like I knew there was no rewinding the hands of time. You had to either keep pushing on or get pushed on.

"How long will it take you to get here?" I asked.

"I gotta check flight times, but - "

"No, you don't, my plane is still at LAX," I said quickly.

"It is? Well, alright now. I'm up in Oakland handling some business, but if you can send it this way, I'll have me and my people their ASAP."

The feeling of relief was so intense that I collapsed backwards on the bed, silent tears pouring from my eyes.

"Th-thank you so much, thank - "

"Stop all that, Ebony. I'm still the same nigga you knew from when we were young and dumb. I'm just older, wiser and sexier. But I'll always be loyal, and I promised you a long time ago that if you ever needed me, I'd be there. I'm on the way," he said sincerely.

"I'll take care of the plane," I said, hanging up before I embarrassed myself by ugly crying with him on the phone.

We were each other's first love, the first everything in a lot of ways, but right now I felt like he was my savior. And I damn sure needed one.

I set about the business of making sure the travel was straight, and once that was done, I set my mind towards a strategy that would result in getting my mom and Rock back and killing Ivy. Things could never be what they were, so it was either her or me.

CHAPTER 20
IVY

"I need to know where that picture was taken."

"Ivy, you've been saying the same thing for hours, and for hours I've been telling you that I've got the best people I know working on it," Joey said, exasperated.

I started to cuss his ass out, considering that I had to add onto his normal fee just to get him to drop everything and come to my house. The least he could do as my lawyer was earn the goddamn money!

"Time is something I don't have, but you seem not to understand that," I said, gripping the Glock .17 in my hand tighter.

"And shooting me ain't gonna make shit happen any faster, Ivy. I want your father home too. I mean for God's sake, I thought he was lost to us forever. I'm telling you, if we send the picture to the FBI, then - "

"No cops," Hoover Slim reiterated from his relaxed position on my couch.

Part of me wanted to side with my lawyer because I understood the governments resources were limitless, but I was too deep in the game now to play it straight.

"What about your people, Slim?" I asked.

"I got the word out, and I put a call in to Gangsta Bit, but he thought your pops was dead too."

"That nigga is probably lying," I said, becoming more furious as more time passed.

"Yeah, he could be, but I don't believe he is so we gotta wait until I hear something," he replied calmly.

I wanted to shoot him right in his fucking forehead for his icy calm, but that was definitely counterproductive at this point. Being in the same room with him made it too tempting though, so I walked out. My intention had been to find another room to pace in, but before I knew it I was in the garage inside my Aston Martin, backing it out and smoking the tires as I peeled away.

I had no destination in mind, so I just let the power and speed of my car eat up the road in front of me. I felt like there were just too many emotions inside me fighting for dominance, and I didn't know which one to let through, but if I didn't decide, I'd be destroyed. Everything that I'd done or justified being done was because my dad was taken and killed. So to know that he was alive, even though he was obviously hurt because he was laid up in a hospital bed, had me questioning every move I'd made. Would my father have made the same decisions I did? I had to believe that he would've because losing me would've been just as devastating to him as his loss was to me. What I had doubts about was how he would've handled Jacob and his family.

Soon my little joy ride had me flying down a little two lane back road that ended with a wide open pasture that was fenced in. I couldn't remember the last time I'd been here, but my family had owned the land for as long as I'd been alive. Sitting in my car looking through the windshield I could see the six-year-old version of myself, riding my first pony in the bright sunshine of summer mornings. I loved being here. It was so peaceful, and my dad always had to fight to get me to leave even when dusk had come and gone. Ebony was the same way. Riding our ponies together was the only thing that could get us away from our tea parties and baby dolls because we both loved animals, even more than that we loved each other.

So how in the hell had shit gone so wrong that death for either one of us seemed like the only way out? It was madness to think that the woman who'd cooked me many meals and kissed every booboo I'd ever had, even if my own mom had already kissed them, was now held captive in my house. The truth was that Ebony and I had both gone mad, and this sentimental trip down memory lane couldn't change that.

Putting my car in reverse, I backed out of the past and pointed myself in the direction of the very uncertain future. It made no sense to get me and my dad killed, and the fact that Ebony wanted me to show up alone told me that her plan was exactly that. It seemed like despite our no longer being close we still agreed on what was important. One of us had to die tonight. I drove back home with more organization to the chaos in my mind, putting things into perspective to ensure that survival was still my motivation. I walked into the house to find everybody pretty much in the same position I'd left them in.

"It's not smart or safe to run off by yourself, even if you do have a gun," Slim said, clearly annoyed.

"I needed to think. Have either of you heard anything?" I asked.

"Not yet," Joey replied.

"Okay, well it's not important where my dad is now because it's too late in the day to organize a rescue mission before the meeting. We gotta focus on the meeting itself because you can bet that she's not trying to let me walk away alive," I said.

"Now you're thinking. I've already got the spot staked out by my people, so we'll know when she gets there, and who she's with," Slim said.

"We know it was the Sinaloa Cartel that took my father, so it stands to reason that they'll back whatever Ebony's play is. I still don't understand why they kept him alive," I wondered, aloud.

"Leverage. You don't give up your only leverage," Slim stated simply.

His statement gave an idea in my mind life, forcing me to stand here in silence while it took shape. There was no doubt in my mind that Ebony planned to take me and my father out once she got what she wanted, but I wouldn't make it easy for her. I still had leverage.

CHAPTER 21
EBONY

"It's good to see you," I said, folding comfortably into his 6'2" frame when he hugged me.

Aside from cutting his long hair and putting on about twenty pounds of solid muscle, Justice was still the same light-skinned pretty boy with the easy smile. That smile was deceiving though because I knew he was with the bullshit at a moment's notice.

"It's good seeing you too, although I wish it was under better circumstances," he replied, following me into my hotel room.

"Me too. Did your people get set up down the hall?"

"I guess. I mean, I gave the niggas the room numbers and told them not to break shit. You would've thought they were the Golden State Warriors after the championship with the way they were acting on that damn plane," he said, shaking his head.

I wasn't surprised to hear this considering that Justice was known to surround himself with real street niggas, most of whom had probably never been out of Cali. I had no doubts that they knew how to get the job done though.

"A'ight, so tell me what you couldn't tell me on the phone," he said, sitting beside me on the couch.

It wasn't like I'd kept anything from him, but you always had to be careful how you spoke because you never knew who was listening.

"Ivy killed my dad - shot him in the back of the head while someone recorded it."

"Wow. If anybody except you was telling me this, I'd say hell nah, but wow," he replied, clearly stunned.

"Yeah, me too. After that I lost it, and I shot up her mom's funeral."

I thought he might not have heard me because he just stared at me, blinking real slowly.

"After that - "

"Wait, wait, you can't just say you casually shot up your best friend's mom's funeral, a woman that you loved like a mom too by the way," he said, obviously concerned.

"Things are different now, J. we're not a family anymore, and there's been too much that has happened to ever get that back."

"Okay, I understand that, but that don't mean you don't feel some type of way about all this shit," he said.

"Feel? I can't feel. I'm not allowed to feel, and you know that."

I knew he wanted to argue, and back in the day he probably would've, but he knew the truth when he heard it. There were no feelings in the street. You had to be colder than the morgue or you'd end up there.

"You know I got love for you, but I need you to keep it 100 with me. Did you bring me out here to kill Ivy?" he asked, searching my face like he was trying to peer into my soul.

"I wouldn't do that to you, Justice. I know you have love for her too despite the history you and I share. I'ma kill her myself," I replied honestly.

In my heart I know Justice loved me enough to take this burden from me and put Ivy in the ground, but I couldn't ask that of him. This was my fight.

"There has to be another way. I mean - "

"If I don't kill her, she's gonna kill us - me, and my baby," I said softly.

Hearing the news about me being pregnant made Justice sit back on the couch and cover his face with his hands. I had no idea what was going through his mind right now, but I knew it wasn't judgement.

"Does Rockafella know?" he asked.

"Yes," I replied, glad at least one person in my life didn't question if I was stingy with the pussy or not.

"A'ight then. Well tell me what your plan is."

"I don't really have one except to get my mom and Rock back and come out guns blazing. My associate in the Sinaloa Cartel will touch down with Ivy's dad in a couple hours, and then - "

"Whoa, back up, I thought Ivy's dad was dead," he said, leaning forward again.

"Yeah, that's what everyone thought, but the cartel had him the whole time, thanks to my father's betrayal. They probably would've returned him just to put an end to the war they were losing, but shit went sideways and Soloman almost died. He's alive, but he's paralyzed from the neck down."

"So, you're trading him to get your family back. Okay, but explain to me how the fuck Ivy wins in a war with both the Sinaloa Cartel and Global Gangstas?" he asked.

"Because she went into business with the Gulf Cartel, and Big Cuzz is a Hoover. My dad's power play backfired because the legal business shields the illegal money and merchandise that come through the ports, and those businesses were controlled by Soloman went missing. Ivy's mom had a heart attack, and that left Ivy in charge. She made her move before my dad could, and then she took total control of the business. I've been fighting her, but controlling the ports essentially controls everything so she has no shortage of 'friends' to help her."

"Sounds like I'm gonna need more people," he said, pulling out his phone and walking to the balcony.

I hadn't lied to him during our first phone call, but it was kinda hard to explain how real shit was over the phone. The fact that he was calling for reinforcements meant he fully understood what we were going up against, but time was getting short. It was ten minutes before he came back inside and sat down beside me.

"I called in a few favors and my niggas from Dallas are on their way out here."

"I can send my plane if - "

"Nah, they're travelling way too deep for that, plus they got big tools. Don't worry though because they'll be here in plenty of time," he assured.

"Thank you, Justice. I don't know what else to say."

"I just need you to be sure that this is what you wanna do because once bullets start flying, you can't change your mind," he warned.

"I'm sure. There ain't no way around it, so it's on."

CHAPTER 22
IVY
12:01 A.M.

"'Bout time you stop hiding from me," I said, leaning against the hood of the Phantom with the Glock in my hand on full display.

"Hiding? Bitch, you ain't built like that. Heads up: I'll beat your ass and you know it," she replied, assuming the same position on the hood of her black Escalade, a familiar-looking nickel plated .45 in her hand.

We both had our headlights on, and that meant she saw nobody in my car just like I saw nobody in her truck. We were alone out here in the middle of the field, but both of us knew that was bullshit.

"You gonna keep lolly popping or we gonna do what we came out here to do?" I asked, fighting the temptation to put a hole in this bitch right now.

"Show me mine and I'll show you yours," she said.

I didn't mind going first since I had twice the head count, so I went to the truck and opened it. I could feel the heat from the hateful glare Marissa was giving me, but I locked all emotion away and pulled her from the trunk.

"Walk slow because if you run I'll shoot you down where you stand," I warned, pushing her towards the front of my car.

"Where's Rock?" Ebony asked.

"I believe it's your turn," I said, grabbing her mom by the hair and sticking my gun to the back of her head.

She quickly pulled her phone out and sent a text. Minutes later I heard a vehicle approaching and then a truck came into view, parking behind hers. The driver got out and went to the truck, and then reappeared with a body slung over his shoulder like he was a fireman. From the photo I was sent I knew something was wrong with my dad because he'd been laid in a hospital bed hooked up to monitors, but if they were just bringing me his body, then everybody would die now. I thought seeing my father's face as he was laid next to my car would surprise me, but the bigger shock was the nigga carrying him.

"J-Justice," I said, unable to keep the awe out of my voice.

"Long time no see," he replied.

"Wh-what are you doing here? I thought you were back in Cali," I said, stammering and still unable to believe what I was seeing.

Justice was about three years older than Ebony, but we all went back to when we were young, dumb teenagers. Aside from Big, Justice has always been the realest nigga I ever knew. He'd always been there for me and Ebony, even though they'd ended up becoming a couple for a while. I was never jealous of their relationship though, which was why I'd never told Ebony that I'd sampled the dick too. He was both of our firsts, but only him and I knew that. Shit, it had been my pussy he practiced eating on the regular so he could get good enough to impress Ebony. Seeing him here now, with her, was bittersweet, to say the least.

"I came down here because our friend called me. I admit, I thought she might've been exaggerating how bad shit had gone between you too, but the fact that you've got a gun to Marissa's head right now speaks volumes," he said.

"And the fact that you just carried my dad over here doesn't?" I countered.

"This wasn't Ebony's doing. You know that."

"I don't know anything. What's wrong with him?" I asked, studying the slow rise and fall of his chest, which at least indicated he was alive.

"He's sedated. And he's paralyzed from the neck down."

I couldn't keep the sudden gasp that escaped from my mouth locked in, but I quickly put my hurt away and latched on to my anger. Swiftly I smacked Marissa over the head with my gun, knocking her out and pushing her to the ground.

"Bitch!" Ebony yelled, advancing on me with her gun leveled at my face.

I simply gave her a knowing smile, tucked my gun into the waist of my jeans, and grabbed my dad under his arms so I could drag him to the back of the car. Once I had him comfortable in the backseat I returned to see that Justice had disappeared with Marissa, leaving just me and Ebony again.

"Give me Rock," she demanded, still pointing her gun at me.

"Or what? You gonna shoot me?" I asked, pulling my own gun and pointing it back at her.

"If you don't hand Rock over you won't make it out of here alive."

"And if you shoot me you'll never see him again, so put your gun away and tell whoever Justice brought with him to stand down," I said.

"What makes you think I came with anyone?" Justice asked, rejoining us, this time with a chrome 9mm Beretta in his hand.

"Because I know you and you didn't come down here to mediate, nigga. You came for your precious Ebony. The fact that you're even holding a gun right now says it all," I replied, hating the betrayal I felt in this moment.

"I'm just here to keep everybody honest," he said.

"Honest? Do you even know what that word means? If you do, then Ebony probably already knows that you learned how to eat pussy by snacking on mine damn near every day, right?" I asked, smiling.

I knew I was the queen of petty for bringing that up right now, but the look of surprise and disbelief on Ebony's face was worth it.

"He never touched you, bitch," Ebony spat.

"Do you hear that? I damn sure don't hear no objections coming from his mouth," I said, laughing now.

"None of that old shit matters. Where's Rockafella?" Justice asked.

In response I lowered my gun and headed for the driver's side of the car, preparing to leave.

"Bitch, if you take another step, your head is gonna explode," Ebony threatened.

I stopped in my tracks and turned around to face her.

"Do it," I challenged.

"Yes, do it," a voice called, out of the dark. I didn't know who the voice belonged to, but she obviously did because she didn't seem surprised in the slightest. Suddenly out of the pitch black appeared a figure to my left, holding a gun of his own.

"What are you waiting for? Shoot her," he ordered.

"José, I don't have Rock yet," Ebony said.

"You're José?" I said, pointing my gun in his direction.

"You're pathetic," he said, raising his gun and pointing it at Ebony.

The difference between his movement and mine was that when he pointed his gun, I heard an array of other weapons being cocked simultaneously. This mu'fucka definitely had back up, and from the sound of it, they had us surrounded.

"What the fuck are you doing pointing the gun at her? She's pregnant," Justice said, standing in front of Ebony.

I knew my mouth was hanging open, but I couldn't help that because the surprises just kept coming.

"She is weak. They both are. They need to be eliminated so my people can take over, and I don't mind going through you to get to either of them," José declared.

A quick glance in Ebony's direction revealed that this wasn't going how she thought it would, but I wasn't surprised because rule number one was trust no one. Out of the shadows I could feel the presence of people pressing in on us, which meant shit was about to hit the fan.

"Ebony," I said, again looking in her direction. She looked like a deer in headlights, but it was too late for that now.

I had time to blink once, and then the night came alive with gunfire.

To Be Continued...
What Bad Bitches Do 2
Coming Soon

Submission Guideline.

Submit the first three chapters of your completed manuscript to ldpsubmissions@gmail.com, subject line: Your book's title. The manuscript must be in a .doc file and sent as an attachment. Document should be in Times New Roman, double spaced and in size 12 font. Also, provide your synopsis and full contact information. If sending multiple submissions, they must each be in a separate email.

Have a story but no way to send it electronically? You can still submit to LDP/Ca$h Presents. Send in the first three chapters, written or typed, of your completed manuscript to:

LDP: Submissions Dept
Po Box 870494
Mesquite, Tx 75187

DO NOT send original manuscript. Must be a duplicate.

Provide your synopsis and a cover letter containing your full contact information.

Thanks for considering LDP and Ca$h Presents.

Coming Soon from Lock Down Publications/Ca$h Presents

BOW DOWN TO MY GANGSTA

By **Ca$h**

TORN BETWEEN TWO

By **Coffee**

BLOOD STAINS OF A SHOTTA **III**

By **Jamaica**

WHEN THE STREETS CLAP BACK **III**

By **Jibril Williams**

STEADY MOBBIN

By **Marcellus Allen**

BLOOD OF A BOSS **V**

By **Askari**

LOYAL TO THE GAME **IV**

By **T.J. & Jelissa**

A DOPEBOY'S PRAYER **II**

By **Eddie "Wolf" Lee**

IF LOVING YOU IS WRONG… **III**

LOVE ME EVEN WHEN IT HURTS

By **Jelissa**

DAUGHTERS OF A SAVAGE

By **Chris Green**

SKI MASK CARTEL **II**

By **T.J. Edwards**

TRAPHOUSE KING

By **Hood Rich**

BLAST FOR ME **II**

RAISED AS A GOON **V**

By **Ghost**

A DISTINGUISHED THUG STOLE MY HEART **III**

By **Meesha**

ADDICTIED TO THE DRAMA **III**

By **Jamila Mathis**

LIPSTICK KILLAH **II**

By **Mimi**

WHAT BAD BITCHES DO 2

By **Aryanna**

THE COST OF LOYALTY **II**

By **Kweli**

A DRUG KING AND HIS DIAMOND **II**

By **Nicole Goosby**

Available Now

RESTRAINING ORDER **I & II**

By **CA$H & Coffee**

LOVE KNOWS NO BOUNDARIES **I II & III**

By **Coffee**

RAISED AS A GOON I, II, III & IV

BRED BY THE SLUMS I, II, III

BLAST FOR ME

By **Ghost**

LAY IT DOWN **I & II**

LAST OF A DYING BREED

BLOOD STAINS OF A SHOTTA I & II

By **Jamaica**

LOYAL TO THE GAME

LOYAL TO THE GAME II

LOYAL TO THE GAME III

By **TJ & Jelissa**

BLOODY COMMAS I & II

SKI MASK CARTEL

By **T.J. Edwards**

IF LOVING HIM IS WRONG…I & II

By **Jelissa**

WHEN THE STREETS CLAP BACK I & II

By **Jibril Williams**

A DISTINGUISHED THUG STOLE MY HEART I & II

By **Meesha**

PUSH IT TO THE LIMIT

By **Bre' Hayes**

BLOOD OF A BOSS **I, II, III & IV**

By **Askari**

THE STREETS BLEED MURDER **I, II & III**

THE HEART OF A GANGSTA I II& III

By **Jerry Jackson**

CUM FOR ME

CUM FOR ME 2

CUM FOR ME 3

An **LDP Erotica Collaboration**

BRIDE OF A HUSTLA **I & II**

THE FETTI GIRLS **I, II& III**

By **Destiny Skai**

WHEN A GOOD GIRL GOES BAD

By **Adrienne**

A GANGSTER'S REVENGE **I II III & IV**

THE BOSS MAN'S DAUGHTERS

THE BOSS MAN'S DAUGHTERS II

THE BOSSMAN'S DAUGHTERS III

THE BOSSMAN'S DAUGHTERS IV

A SAVAGE LOVE **I & II**

BAE BELONGS TO ME

A HUSTLER'S DECEIT I, II

By **Aryanna**

A KINGPIN'S AMBITON

A KINGPIN'S AMBITION **II**

I MURDER FOR THE DOUGH

By **Ambitious**

TRUE SAVAGE

TRUE SAVAGE II

TRUE SAVAGE **III**

By **Chris Green**

A DOPEBOY'S PRAYER

By **Eddie "Wolf" Lee**

THE KING CARTEL **I, II & III**

By **Frank Gresham**

THESE NIGGAS AIN'T LOYAL **I, II & III**

By **Nikki Tee**

GANGSTA SHYT **I II &III**

By **CATO**

THE ULTIMATE BETRAYAL

By **Phoenix**

BOSS'N UP **I , II & III**

By **Royal Nicole**

I LOVE YOU TO DEATH

By Destiny J

I RIDE FOR MY HITTA

I STILL RIDE FOR MY HITTA

By **Misty Holt**

LOVE & CHASIN' PAPER

By **Qay Crockett**

TO DIE IN VAIN

By **ASAD**

BROOKLYN HUSTLAZ

By **Boogsy Morina**

BROOKLYN ON LOCK I & II

By **Sonovia**

GANGSTA CITY

By **Teddy Duke**

A DRUG KING AND HIS DIAMOND

A DOPEMAN'S RICHES

By Nicole Goosby

BOOKS BY LDP'S CEO, CA$H

TRUST IN NO MAN

TRUST IN NO MAN 2

TRUST IN NO MAN 3

BONDED BY BLOOD

SHORTY GOT A THUG

THUGS CRY

THUGS CRY 2

THUGS CRY 3

TRUST NO BITCH

TRUST NO BITCH 2

TRUST NO BITCH 3

TIL MY CASKET DROPS

RESTRAINING ORDER

RESTRAINING ORDER 2

IN LOVE WITH A CONVICT

Coming Soon

BONDED BY BLOOD 2

BOW DOWN TO MY GANGSTA

CPSIA information can be obtained
at www.ICGtesting.com
Printed in the USA
LVHW031541231121
704247LV00012B/1373